Sitting in the outer office, Rebecca nervously waited to be called in for the job interview that might secure her new life.

Just then a male voice came over the intercom. Rebecca didn't quite know why she jumped at the voice, but her heart somersaulted in her chest.

"Send Ms. Wood in."

Gripping the door knob, Rebecca turned it and pushed the door open. Her eyes widened in horror at what awaited her.

The employer on the other side of the monstrous desk glared at her with familiar blue eyes while a mocking grin tugged at his lips. Rebecca felt herself swoon as she recognized the driver of the black Mercedes, Trevor Houston, the man she had hit that early morning at the gas pump in Dallas.

KELLY R. STEVENS lives in Texas with her husband and two children. In her writing, Kelly wants to "draw on real issues" and show that "the wonder of giving love and receiving love comes from God." *Ragdoll* is Kelly's inspirational romance debut.

Ragdoll

Kelly R. Stevens

Heartsong Presents

Dedication

This book is dedicated to Doris and Virgil Varner, my mother and father, for never failing to trust in my vision.

Acknowledgements

Many thanks go to these people for their help and support during the writing of this book: Doris Varner, Mike Hartsock, Linda Pope, Marie McNutt, and Kelly McElwain.

A note from the Author:

I love to hear from my readers! You may write to me at the following address:

Kelly R. Stevens
Author Relations
P.O. Box 719
Uhrichsville, OH 44683

ISBN 1-55748-661-1

RAGDOLL

PRINTED IN THE U.S.A.

prologue

Helena could do nothing more. Arrangements had already been made. It was for the best, she reasoned. Yet she couldn't control the trickle of tears that left silvery, wet paths down her pale cheeks.

Glimpsing across the room the skeletal figure covered by a thin white sheet, she realized it has been days since her husband had moved. Huge breaths escaped out of his lungs with a gurgle. Helena knew that Lyle would leave her soon.

Rocking back and forth in the rocker, her gaze moved to the tiny bundle held in her arms: an infant barely four days old. The birth certificate held the date, January 10, 1972, but no name.

Her newborn daughter's pink lips contentedly nursed at Helena's swollen breast. Helena smiled as she watched the baby slip repeatedly into short naps before sucking hungrily again.

The delivery had gone well. For this, Helena was grateful. She hated leaving Lyle alone in his fragile condition, but her older daughter, Danielle, had taken good care of him.

At thirteen, Danielle was such a strength to her, helping to take care of three-year-old Denise while most of Helena's attention was devoted to Lyle. No wonder she loved them so. And how she loved the child she now held. That was why she would do what she must. She prayed Lyle would understand.

Helena recalled the day she realized something was not right with her husband. Of course, Lyle would never complain. But he couldn't hide the weight loss, or the time she saw him leaning against the shed, holding his gut, extreme pain etched in his features. Then he missed three days of work at the construction site of a new home. Finally, he'd let her call the doctor.

After blood tests and x-rays, the doctor spent a long time in the clinic's office with Lyle while Helena paced the floor outside the door. The shock of the diagnosis, when the doctor finally came out, still haunted her seven months later.

"Cancer," the doctor muttered as he made notations on a pad of paper attached to a clipboard. She remembered that he avoided her eyes, and Lyle's.

"Get your affairs in order," he whispered while they were filing out the door, seemingly anxious to be done with them.

The doctor never billed them. But that had been the least of her worries. At the time, she was two months pregnant with their third child. How could she live without Lyle? How could she raise their daughters and make a life for them? She barely managed now.

Helena smiled for a second as she watched the baby's face squeeze into a grimace. She laid the tiny bundle of life over her shoulder and began a series of gentle pats on its bottom. This was nothing new to her. The only difference was that Lyle was not beside her, his eyes filled with tears at the sight of their newest miracle.

The baby passed a good burp and fell asleep on Helena's shoulder. She cradled the tiny infant in her arms and watched the soft, sweet breaths, glad she had arranged things so this brief time could be spent with her baby. Neither the adoption agency nor its appointed lawyers felt it was a good idea. They said it was not "proper procedure." But Helena wouldn't have it any other way.

Studying the baby's features, Helena ran her slender fingers through the downy crown of dark hair, so different from the last two. They were more like her, blond and pale. This baby's hair was thicker with brilliant red highlights that shifted in the light, like Lyle's.

She touched a fingertip gently over the rows of long, dark lashes that framed lucent green eyes and allowed the finger to caress the creamy, olive skin of the baby's cheeks. Tears ran unrestrained down Helena's face.

"You're so beautiful," she whispered as though the infant could understand. "Your daddy would be so proud of you." She peered again at the still figure under the sheet. "I bet you'd like to meet your daddy, wouldn't you?"

Helena stood with the baby still cradled in her arms. Soreness from the painful delivery caused her to step very carefully to her husband's bedside where he lay in a deep, coma-like sleep.

Placing the sleeping baby on the pillow beside him, she watched them silently for a while, marveling at the fact that they were so close together and yet so oblivious to each other. How she would miss them both, she thought, when they were gone! Her bottom lip quivered and fresh tears stung her eyes as she began the introduction.

"Lyle Warren Lindley, this is your new daughter," said

Helena, in a voice racked by tears. The dying man did not stir. "I didn't know what to name her," she continued. "We always did that part together." Helena caressed her husband's pale forehead. "And daughter," Helena smiled through her tears, "this is your daddy."

She observed them both for a time and then left them to sleep while she collected the baby's things. It would not be long.

Helena approached an old trunk pressed against a far wall of the shabby, two-room apartment. Lifting the groaning lid, she dug through tattered hand-me-downs until she found a pale green sleeper with faded pink bows that would fit the infant.

Next, she hunted for a suitable blanket to guard the baby against the blasts of cold winter air. The thin receiving blanket wrapped around the baby simply would not do.

She pulled out an old pair of button shoes with dull kid tops that had belonged to her grandmother, a darning ball for socks, and an incomplete set of ivory-handled silverware from the chest. Then Helena reached the quilt; a worn, hand-sewn wedding gift from her mother, scattered with mauve, yellow, and green dutch girls over its face. She chuckled. The quilt was so ragged from years of use that she decided the pattern better resembled rag dolls than its original Dutch girl pattern. "This will work just fine," she said aloud.

Helena had just placed the quilt to her face, drinking in the musty odors of the cedar chest that permeated the blanket's fibers, when something in the chest caught her eye.

Lifting the glimmering object from the wooden box,

she placed it gently in the palm of her hand. The gold alloy was dulled by time and the natural oils of her husband's hands.

Roman numerals peered back at her from beneath the scratched glass face. The pocket watch had been passed down to Lyle forty-two years ago from his father, at Lyle's birth. The Elgin watch had been in the family since 1875, and Helena regarded it as one of their true treasures. Lyle had hoped to give the watch to his son, but they had been blessed with three girls.

The initials L.W.L. were engraved on the inside. Helena knew that the watch must go to their new daughter. She knew that Lyle would want it this way.

With trembling fingers, Helena turned the key wind and freed the delicate melody from its music-box prison. Helena set the watch at 2:10 p.m. and wound the second key wind. It ticked perfectly.

Helena gave herself a mental shake. She walked over to the bed, picked up the baby, and wrapped her in the quilt, smiling as the infant all but disappeared in the blanket's large folds. Just then a knock sounded on the door.

Helena felt a knot rise in her throat. Opening the door, she saw a man dressed in a black business suit and two women in drab dresses and gray wool overcoats. There were no smiles with their greetings as they stepped into the apartment.

"Is this the child?" asked one of the women. Helena said nothing as she handed the bundle over to the woman. "Boy, or girl?" asked the woman, raising a fold of the quilt to expose the baby's face.

"Girl." Helena spoke in a low voice, nearly choking

on the word. The woman placed the bundle securely in the cook of her arm and turned toward the door. The others followed silently.

Before they could leave, Helena touched the elbow of the woman who held her baby. Their gazes met and for a moment she almost grabbed the child away. But Helena knew that would be selfish of her. Her child deserved better than she could offer her.

She grasped the woman's hand and placed the pocket watch firmly in her palm. "For the baby," she choked, "from her father."

Standing in the doorway, she clung weakly to the shoddy frame as she watched her daughter be carried away. Tears stung her eyes and her heart throbbed in pain for her daughter.

"Good bye, my little ragdoll," she whispered as she watched the blue sedan drive away.

one

Houston, Texas, 1983

Rebecca giggled as her father tousled her thick mane of auburn hair. Sitting on his lap, she reached up with a slender hand and tugged playfully on one end of his mustache, her laughing mouth opened wide, showing two rows of perfect teeth.

Not a day went by that Rebecca didn't greet her father as he stepped through the door, like a habit that can't be denied.

Although only ten years old, Rebecca was well aware of the calming effect she had on her dad. When she hugged him, she never released her grip until his shoulders relaxed against the pressure of the hug.

Rebecca burst into another laugh as her father tickled her ribs. Both froze, however, when her mother stamped into the reception hall, a rolled newspaper gripped tightly in her white-knuckled hand. Rebecca rose from her father's lap and stood statue-still.

"How did your tennis lessons go today?" Candace asked sternly, a deep southern drawl rolling with the words off her lips. She studied the two of them with cold, gray eyes.

"F. . .fine." Rebecca cast her green gaze down. She knew there would be more. There always was. Her mother's only concern was Rebecca's tennis lessons. That fact pierced the girl's heart like a bullet. She wanted to cry out, "What about school? What about my friends? What about me?"

Her mother lodged her hands on her hips in one deliberate motion. "That's not what Tatianna tells me!"

"What?" Rebecca asked innocently.

"What does Tatianna know?" interjected Rebecca's father. "I don't approve of her tattling!"

Candace's face flushed as Shane Wesbrook continued. "Rebecca's not interested in the game in the first place! Our daughter wants to join gymnastics! Why can't you accept that?"

Candace's voice catapulted like a vaulter. "Tatianna knows what's she's talkin' about!"

Rebecca didn't move, knowing they were in for another tense evening. Her mother's silence would be played out over supper and possibly for days. She wished she could eat with Maria, their live-in maid and nanny.

"How does Tatianna know what she's talking about?" Shane asked in a quiet, stern voice.

"She says our Rebecca could turn pro if she would put more effort into the game and that Rebecca has more athletic ability than any of her other students!"

Rebecca wanted to tell her mother that she could be just as good at gymnastics—better—but she knew not to cross her mother when she was in this mood.

Candace splayed the Houston paper open to the sports section before slapping it down on her husband's lap. Pointing to a picture of a woman poised with a tennis racket, she spouted, "It's Chris Evert."

"What about her?" Shane briefly scanned the photo.

Candace tapped a long, polished nail against the black and white shot. "She just won the Virginia Slims tournament, that's what! That's where our daughter could be five years from now if you'd teach her 'bout strivin' for whatcha want outta life!"

"You mean what you want," Shane muttered.

Candace pretended not to hear.

Shane gripped the handle of his leather briefcase that rested atop an occasional table beside the chair. The decorative Princeton oil lamp that graced its top shook as he removed the case and stood, letting the newspaper drop with a thud to the floor.

Steadying the table, Candace shouted, "Watch it!"

"Do your antiques mean more to you than your daughter? What's happened to you?" His tone softened. "What's happened to my beautiful bride? What monster has driven you from us?"

Rebecca glanced quizzically in her mother's direction, wondering again at her unusual beauty.

Although thirty-nine, Candace had natural blond hair that framed delicate ivory features. Mysterious gray eyes, turned cold and empty, had once been the highlight of her porcelain-doll beauty.

Rebecca knew that her mother's attitude wasn't normal. She often wondered what she could have done to cause her mother to be so displeased with her and had once overheard her father talking to Maria quietly about the same question.

"What went wrong?" he had asked. Rebecca remembered the evening well.

Finishing her homework early, Rebecca had bounded down the stairs in search of her father and Maria. She'd overheard their hushed whispers and the quake in her father's voice as they talked in the dining hall.

"She never said no," he confided to Maria who always made time to listen to his troubles and had become more a close friend than an employee. "I thought she'd be as thrilled as I when the baby came."

Rebecca crouched low by a north wall, listening, hoping to glean some understanding herself. She knew it was wrong to eavesdrop, but she couldn't help herself. She was as desperate as her father to know what went wrong.

Rebecca overheard words she didn't understand, like *infertility.* Her father confided to Maria about all the money they had spent trying to fix an infertility problem, and how several doctors had told them that nothing was wrong physically.

Her father had told Maria that he felt sorry about his wife's obsession to bear a child, Rebecca remembered, although she didn't understand why a woman would want something like that so badly. Wasn't it painful? She remembered thinking that maybe she had hurt her mother and that was the reason she was mad all the time.

Rebecca's father went on to recall how they'd brought her home as an infant, wrapped in an old quilt. She heard him describe to Maria how excited her mother had been about all the attention lavished on her and the infant. "With all the attention, Candace seemed content. She played the perfect part of the doting mother. Our lives finally came together."

Their happiness didn't last, Rebecca's father said. Soon, his wife grew restless. It seemed the baby became more of an imposition to her than a gift. That's when he stepped in. The only thing he could do was hire a full-time nanny. Rebecca was less than a year old when Maria came.

Rebecca listened as her father described her mother's

new life. She surrounded herself with friends, diving into a social life that he could be not part of, a social life that meant late nights and drinking binges. The only thing that piqued his wife's interest toward her daughter, he explained to Maria, was her tennis game. No one knew why.

Rebecca remembered Maria simply nodded with compassion and understanding. It was then Rebecca had stood from her crouched position and stepped into the dining room. She plopped herself on her father's lap, acting as though she had just arrived.

At times, Rebecca felt crushed by her mother's disinterest but the loving attention showered on her from Maria and her father more than made up for it. She was unusually happy.

Rebecca had developed a levelheaded business sense that she knew pleased her father. Here, she took after him, and he wasted no time teaching her about finances, investments, smart moves and bad. As owner and president of Financial Investment Security Services, FISS, Shane Wesbrook believed in what he did: helping individuals and corporations achieve financial security through counseling, investment planning, and action. He managed a group of prosperous companies nationwide that his father had created and then willed to Shane upon his death in 1969.

Rebecca's business vocabulary was better than many of FISS's newly hired employees. It showed in her grades at school. She was strong in all her subjects at Coronado Christian Academy, especially math. Maria chose the private school. Shane didn't argue the point. Having spent a lot of time with his daughter, Maria knew what was best for her.

"Don't walk away from me when I'm talkin' to you!" Candace yelled.

Rebecca's eyes widened to the size of saucers as she was rushed back into the present. Her father ignored her mother.

"Becca," he murmured, a pet name only he called her, "go get ready for dinner." Before either could leave, Maria came through the sitting room to the right of the reception hall.

"Dinner will be ready in thirty minutes," she said with a thick Spanish accent.

Perfect timing, Rebecca thought. She watched Shane leave the room, taking the stairs that would lead him to his study on the third floor. Her attention went to Maria, gazing lovingly at her nanny who, at forty-five, had no visible lines on her face. Long, ebony hair habitually woven into a neat braid, ran the length of her back. Large, chocolate eyes peered out from above high cheek bones.

Rebecca knew Maria's love was unconditional, a love that warmed the body and touched the soul. For as long as Rebecca could remember, Maria had been there for her needs. If Rebecca had a problem, Maria had an answer or a suggestion or simply time to listen. There were times she had made Rebecca come up with her own solutions.

Rebecca wished she could have as close a relationship with her mother. Her growing faith convinced her that the possibility was there. But when? This was one answer no one could provide.

Maria had tried to explain the problem to her several months earlier, right after a disastrous argument occurred between Rebecca and her mother over a test grade, resulting in Rebecca's being sent to bed early.

"Your mother is very jealous of you." Maria whispered softly as she tucked Rebecca in for the night.

"Why?" Rebecca appealed.

Maria smoothed a strand of hair away from Rebecca's damp forehead and dabbed at the tears that spilled shiny paths down her flushed cheeks. "Of you and your father, *niña*," she finally offered. "She does not like the relationship you have with him. But you must remember that you are not to blame.

"I believe she would like to have a good relationship with your father, but since that has not happened, she resents your closeness with him." Maria cupped Rebecca's chin in her hand. "Do you understand?"

Rebecca nodded. "What can I do to make it better?"

"Maybe nothing," Maria said. "But you must not be angry with her. She is *an espiritu extraviado,* a lost soul."

Rebecca pulled the soft, pink blanket up to her chin. She had grown tired and wanted only to sleep, but Maria had one more thing to add.

"Remember, little one, something good will come out of everything, even if it's bad. You must remember this."

"I will try," Rebecca had murmured through half-closed lids.

Maria turned to leave, tearing Rebecca away from her memories. The young girl realized she'd always loved her mother. But it was all she could do: Love her from a distance.

She brushed past her mother on her way to the stairs and mounted the steps two at a time, completely ignoring the polished oak banister.

After washing up and changing into a pale blue dress, more suitable for dinner than her white cotton tennis outfit, Rebecca bounded down the sweeping staircase and headed for the dining hall.

"Well now, there'sh our little beauty," Rebecca heard the familiar voice say with a drunken slur.

"Thank you, Uncle Kane," she offered politely, feeling slightly uncomfortable as she took her seat beside him.

Kane always made her feel uncomfortable, whether drunk or sober. He was not playful and loving like her other uncles.

Most of his remarks had other meanings that, even if Rebecca couldn't decipher, she knew weren't good. He didn't simply look at the person he spoke to, he glared. Nor was he a welcome visitor to the estate, but he was always there. Instinct told Rebecca to stay away from him. Nobody ever warned her. She just knew.

She did think Kane was quite attractive, or could be, had he not let himself go to alcohol and other unhealthy habits. His wavy, chestnut brown hair went uncombed and the dimple in his chin grew deeper as he dropped more and more weight. His green eyes, once the highlight of his good looks, were now bulgy and bloodshot. He looked well beyond his forty years. She knew what he could have looked like just by looking at her father.

Rebecca sat opposite her mother. Her father presided at the head of the massive oak dining table. Maria removed the lid from the silver serving tray to expose broiled salmon glazed with lemon juice and sweetened with pineapple slices. Other dishes revealed rice and pasta. Maria started to pour iced tea into glasses.

"None for me," Kane spouted, holding his hand over the top of the glass. "Got any brandy?"

Shane breathed deeply with exasperation. "You know where it is," he muttered.

"Why thank you, brother," Kane replied sarcastically. "It puzzles me, ya know," he added as he rose from his chair, swaying when he stood. Maria immediately waved him to sit back down and left the room to get him his brandy. Shane didn't drink. The brandy belonged to their deceased father. Shane just hadn't had the time to dispose of it with the extra load of work he was under. Texas' failing economy made his job more difficult. Against the odds, Shane moved with caution, following his father's teachings of honesty, integrity, and faith.

"All thish," Kane said, waving a thick hand through the air at the interior of the home. The massive dining room set the pattern for the rest of the rooms in the estate. Magnificent tapestries hung from the dining room's natural oak paneling and were set off by polished oak flooring. Highly polished furnishings of oak, cherry, and mahogany graced the rooms throughout the three-story mansion.

Shane seemed to stiffen, expecting more. Their father, William Wayne Wesbrook, had left Shane executor of the will and beneficiary to the family fortune, including the Wesbrook Estate. Shane was also in charge of a trust fund that had been set up for Kane and would only be given to him upon completion of both a detoxification program and a year of proven sobriety. Kane blamed Shane for the "unfortunate error" as he called it.

"Why do you shuppose father would leave everything to you?" Kane quizzed as he had repeatedly in the past.

Shane took a sip of his tea and struggled to remain calm. He hated it when Kane dropped in at dinner time. It was always the same argument.

"You know why," Shane said, setting his tea down and snapping a cloth napkin open in the air before placing it on his lap. "The will explained it."

"Oh I know what it shaid all right," Kane boomed, a fiendish glint in his bloodshot eyes. "It shaid that I'm a drunkard who can't be trusted. It shaid that I can only have my trusht fund when I check into a treatment center." His slur disappeared, as though his anger sobered him.

"When *you* feel confident that I've completed this process, then, and only then, will I get my inheritance, which is a drop in the bucket to what you've gotten!"

Kane slurped more brandy from his glass. "You see, dear brother, it doesn't make sense. I can have a drink now and then if I choose. Secondly, *I* am the older brother. Oh, I know, we're identical twins. How could I forget. The fact remains, *little* brother, I was born twenty minutes before you, and that should account for something!"

Shane suddenly rose to his feet and tossed his napkin on his plate. "I will not argue this again!"

Nobody moved as Shane marched from the room, stomping up the stairs to his study. Snide laughter came from Kane's throat as he dug into his salmon with vigor and, to Rebecca's horror, a smirk tugged at her mother's lips. The meal concluded in silence.

two

Houston, Texas, 1990

"Where have you been?" Shane hissed from his bedroom.

Lying awake in her bed, Rebecca shuddered. She hated this time of night. Her parents' fights were growing in intensity and frequency.

"What business is it of yours?" Candace asked cattily.

"You're my wife! I have a right to know where my wife is, don't I?"

"That, Shane is none of your business. You don't own me."

Shane's tone softened. "I know I don't own you."

"I was with friends," said Candace. "We went out and saw a movie. So quit worryin'. Besides, I can live my life as I see fit, come and go as I please."

"Of course you can," Shane agreed, his reasonable demeanor sounding forced. "But what about responsibilities? What about setting an example for your daughter?"

Rebecca's body stiffened on the crisp white linen sheets, expecting the common retort.

"Don't you mean *your* daughter?"

Covering her face with her feather pillow, Rebecca prayed the darkness would chase away the emptiness in her heart. It had grown painfully obvious over the years that her mother didn't want her. Rebecca never asked why. It was a subject that wasn't discussed, except when Maria broached it lightly, sensing Rebecca's hurt.

She wanted to inform her father that he didn't have to worry about her "impressionable age" as he called it. The sting of her mother's neglect had dulled with time. Maria and her father more than made up for her mother's disinterest.

Maria's influence had helped Rebecca develop her own set of Christian values. At eighteen, she had better morals than most of her friends. And it showed. She had no respect for drug addicts who allowed themselves to be led around like "dogs on leashes," as she labeled it. She knew these qualities were partly responsible for her popularity at Coronado Christian Academy. She was well-liked and respected by her peers and the adults in her life.

Rebecca shoved the pillow away from her face as her father began speaking again. Something in his tone piqued her curiosity.

"Then I think she ought to know," he nearly whispered.

Rebecca threw her long legs over the edge of the bed and tiptoed to the door. Positioning an ear by the door jam, she could hear much better. Her father's bedroom was across the corridor from hers.

"Know what?" her mother asked.

"You know what!" came the sharp reply. "It's what we've discussed over and over. It's time she knew!"

Rebecca drew in a sharp breath. She knew there was some mystery about her life, but every time she had tried to discuss it with her father, he had changed the subject after explaining that 'in due time' she would be told.

Her father's next words brought unexpected hope. "We

can't keep going on like this," he intoned without anger.

"What are you sayin'?" Candace implored. "Are you wantin' a divorce? Imagine what that would do to your daughter. What a fine example to set before her. Isn't that what you've preached all these years: *Example*?"

Hot tears flooded Rebecca's eyes. The hypocrisy of her mother's words brought back a two-year-old memory.

Her mother had thrown a party for the Fourth of July. At one point during the party, Rebecca had overheard her mother talking to two other women. The women complimented her on what a wonderful job she was doing in raising her daughter.

"She is so poised," one gushed. "And she's not the least bit skittish, is she?" another remarked. Rebecca could not believe the words her mother countered with.

"It's been a lot of hard work," she insisted. "But I believe raisin' a child is the most important thing one can do. And neither Shane nor myself have taken the responsibility lightly."

"Well, it certainly shows," one of the women voiced before heading to the buffet.

Her father's stricken words brought Rebecca back to the present.

"I don't even know who you are anymore, Candace. And I don't think we should keep going like this. Why won't you tell me what's wrong?" Shane's plea held genuine concern. "Let me help you. Whatever it is, we can work it out together. You know I love you."

Rebecca said a silent prayer that her mother wouldn't take advantage of her father's vulnerability, yet she knew she would. As the voices outside her door droned on, Rebecca stood up and padded back to bed.

After snuggling between the sheets, she covered her head with the fluffy pink blanket. The childish act made her feel safe. Finally, sleep took her.

❧

Rebecca waved the envelope under her friend's freckled nose during the commencement rehearsal in the school's auditorium. Tomorrow night would be the real thing. Although she had squealed with delight when her gown and cap arrived, it couldn't compare to the elation she felt when she had discovered this letter in the mail.

"What is it?" Briann begged, trying to pry the envelope from Rebecca's slender fingers.

The two had been inseparable since elementary school. Briann was valedictorian of their high school graduating class, and Rebecca, barely below her friend in grade point average, was salutatorian. Briann was also tough competition for Rebecca on the tennis court. Only days earlier, Rebecca had watched her friend graze the asphalt like a gazelle in perfect form, her red hair flashing in the noon sun. Still, Rebecca was the better player and took the match by a small margin.

"Guess," Rebecca teased as names were called in robotic fashion by Principal Stewart over the podium microphone. Hadn't Shane been pleased to learn that Rebecca had received scholarships from ten universities on her grades alone? She wanted to study law. Briann's interest was medicine. Both had every intention of achieving their goals.

Rebecca still struggled with the unpleasantness that resulted after Tatianna's regular reports to her mother about her tennis game. But the scholarships, one of which was to Yale, made it easier to take her mother's reprimands, knowing that in a short time she would walk away from Wesbrook Estate. Of course Rebecca would miss her father and Maria, but they could get together for holidays and other special occasions. She would never leave them out of her life.

"Let me see it," Briann whined. Rebecca slapped the envelope into the palm of Briann's hand. Briann tore the letter out of the envelope and hurriedly scanned its contents.

"Oh my!" Bouncing up and down in her seat like an excited toddler, she screamed, "You got the Yale scholarship!"

Silence filled the auditorium. Rebecca plastered herself against the back of the seat and fought to contain the giggles that threatened. She didn't know which was funnier—her friend or the principal hurling a harsh look their way.

Briann's face turned an unnatural shade of red. Her freckles, usually flattering to her delicate features, mingled with pink splotches over her face and throat. Neither girl breathed until the principal commenced reading names off the list again.

"I can't believe you did that," Rebecca giggled.

"I can't believe I did either. When did you know?" Briann tried to avoid the smirks of nearby students.

"Yesterday." Rebecca replaced the envelope safely into her black, leather clutch before snapping it shut. "How 'bout you?" she queried. "Did you hear anything?" Rebecca knew the answer before Briann spoke.

"Twelve!" Briann exclaimed. "I don't know which one to pick!"

Rebecca knew her friend would make the right

decision, just as she herself would, although carrying it through might be a problem. Her mother didn't think she needed a college education. Suddenly the girls recognized the next name over the loud speaker.

"Here I go," Briann whispered. With a smile and a delicate flick of her hand, she was gone.

Just as Briann departed to walk the stage and mimic receiving her diploma and giving the commencement speech, her empty seat was filled.

"Hi, kiddo," said the husky voice.

Rebecca twisted in the seat. She smiled serenely. "Hi to you." Then added, "Shouldn't you be in your place?"

"Are you kidding? Jimmy Young is at the bottom of the list. They're still on the A's." Then his tone changed. "Haven't seen ya in awhile. Where ya been?"

Rebecca allowed her exasperation to show. "Come on, Jimmy, you already know the answer to that. I don't feel right having a relationship bogged down with rigid rules, as it would surely be if my mother has anything to do with it."

"Speaking of your mother," said Jimmy, "I tried to call a week ago. I could hear you and Maria talking in the background. When I asked for you, she said you weren't at home."

Rebecca shrugged her shoulders. "I think she's been listening in on some of our conversations." Then she saw the disappointment on Jimmy's face. "It has nothing to do with you," she soothed. "I've explained that before." She cleared her throat. "I want you to find a girl who has a decent family life. If we tried to build a relationship with my mother in the picture, it would be a joke!"

"Wait a minute," Jimmy cautioned, one large hand held

up in front of him. "I don't care about that. You're worth it."

"No," Rebecca stated flatly. "I'm doing this for you. It's not fair to you." She took his large masculine hand in hers. "But I do want to be friends. Can't we be friends?"

Jimmy's response was to change the subject, and the two teens talked about a variety of subjects until Briann returned to claim her seat.

Jimmy stood and slowly wove his way through rows of maroon, corduroy seats toward his own.

"Rebecca Wesbrook!" The name crackled over the microphone. Jimmy tossed his head around to look in her direction. She winked at him before scooting down the aisle, dodging knees, then she remembered and swung back around.

"By the way, Dad's hosting a graduation party in my honor tomorrow night. Wanna come?" Rebecca had already invited several friends, including Briann.

"You bet," Jimmy answered, his hazel eyes shimmering.

His eyes had attracted Rebecca to him in the first place, but she thought it unfair to expose him to her problems.

Soon after she had met Jimmy, Rebecca had brought him home to meet her father. Instead her mother met them in the reception hall. What followed still outraged Rebecca.

Her mother had grilled Jimmy with questions like, "What exactly do you want from my daughter?"

"Just her company, ma'am," Jimmy had replied.

"I know what you want," Candace remarked snidely. "I know what you all want! And it has nothing to do with her mind."

Flushed with embarrassment, Rebecca coaxed her friend toward the door, opened it, and pushed him outside. "Sorry about that," she choked as tears threatened.

"What's *her* problem?" he asked.

"I don't have any idea," Rebecca said, shaking her head. She realized then that a relationship would never work. Her mother would eventually tear it down.

Rebecca thought of this as she stepped up to the podium to mimic giving her salutatorian address. Focusing on the podium and the line of students crossing the stage from right to left, she smiled at Jimmy sheepishly before making her way down the aisle and up the steps to the right of the stage. After shaking the assistant principal's right hand with her own, she mocked taking an invisible diploma with the other. As she approached the steps leading down the other side of the stage, she nearly squealed.

Freedom was such a deliciously exciting feeling. And it wouldn't be long before she would experience it. Not long at all.

three

Rebecca smiled at herself through the steam-fogged mirror hanging over the sink. She felt great, having slept well, and was excited about the future. After graduation that evening, she would celebrate into the night with friends and relatives.

Emerging from the steamy bathroom after her shower, Rebecca left a path of wet footprints to the walk-in closet. She pulled out a pair of jeans and a T-shirt.

"Rebecca?" The voice on the other side of the door accompanied a gentle knock.

"Come in, Maria."

Maria bustled about the room. "You slept in this morning," she declared while grabbing handfuls of covers and tugging them toward the head of the bed.

"I'm an adult now," Rebecca teased. She pulled the T-shirt over her head and removed the towel from her head, allowing her damp hair to fall in ringlets down her back.

"Hmmm, an adult now," Maria mocked with a glint in her opaque eyes.

After throwing on her jeans, Rebecca grabbed a pillow, placing it beside the pillow already in place at the head of the bed. Together, Maria and Rebecca pulled the pink bedspread over the bed and tucked the excess under the pillows, forming two perfect mounds.

"I'm graduating." Rebecca laughed, knowing she was

being teased. "And that means I'm an *adult* now."

"But you are so young," Maria countered with a slight raise to one ebony eyebrow. She gathered Rebecca's wet towels and tossed them into the hall.

Giggling, Rebecca stepped into a pair of white sandals and ran a comb through her hair. A glance at Maria brought a look of total dismay to her face. The teasing look on Maria's face had faded. "What's wrong?" Rebecca queried, concern edging her voice.

Maria stepped to Rebecca's side of the bed and sat down, wringing her hands nervously, something Rebecca had seen her do in the past whenever she was upset.

"Did I do something? Say something?" Rebecca asked as she sat down next to her nanny.

"You did nothing, *niña*." Maria cupped her hand under Rebecca's chin and held her gaze. "I love you like you were my own."

A knot formed in Rebecca's throat. She loved Maria too. Maria had been like a mother to her. It was Maria whom Rebecca ran to when she returned from school with a special drawing, a grade report, or a scraped knee. It never dawned on her that Maria would be affected by all that had been going on. Rebecca felt all too selfish as she dabbed at a tear that slipped from one of Maria's doleful eyes.

"I'm just going to college, not the other side of the world," she rang out cheerfully, trying to break the tension that weighed heavy in the room, like the musty air of a cave.

"I know, I know," Maria said, running a slender hand through Rebecca's damp ringlets. "But it will not be the same around here without you." Tears fell in rivers down

Maria's cheeks.

Rebecca had a hard time talking through her own abundant supply of tears. "You are like my own mother," she managed. "I really mean that." She held Maria's liquid gaze with her own. "You have always been there for me, Maria. I can't thank you enough for that, for being there." She wrapped her arms around the Spanish beauty, hugging her tightly.

"Thank you, *niña*," was all Maria could say. For a moment they sat in a silent embrace. When Rebecca released her grip, Maria stood. "*Mucho trabajo,* so much work to do," she said, smiling now. "We have much fun ahead, don't we?"

Rebecca nodded. The earlier sensations of excitement returned as she watched Maria disappear down the sweeping staircase, her arms loaded with laundry.

❧

"I can't believe you almost fell," joked Briann.

Rebecca stepped out of the white gown and removed her hat. She placed the hat with its green and gold tassel gently on her vanity. Briann was stomach-down on Rebecca's bed, her feet propped in the air as she studied the two diplomas nicely encased in book-like fashion, the covering a deep blue. The words Valedictorian and Salutatorian were inscribed in gold lettering just above the name of each girl. Four official signatures adorned the bottom.

"I stepped on the gown is all, Briann." Rebecca smiled.

"I've never heard of anyone falling *up* the steps!" Briann retorted before she was engulfed in giggles.

That had been the only glitch to the hour-long ceremony. As far as Rebecca was concerned, the rest of the evening went perfectly. Emotions imbued the entire ceremony and hugs made the rounds in generous numbers, so generous, in fact, that Rebecca's shoulders ached. But she was happy, more happy than she had ever been. She vowed she would never forget this day.

"Can you believe we made it?" Briann asked once she had control of her giggles. "*We made it!*" she repeated.

"It's hard to believe," Rebecca agreed. "I never thought I'd see this day."

Suddenly, Briann left the room and tiptoed down the staircase, far enough to get a good glimpse into the foyer. Then she ran up the stairs as hard and fast as she could.

"There are so many caterers coming and going, that there's not going to be any room for the guests!" she squealed.

Rebecca only laughed as her friend twirled circles around the room, her arms extended as though dancing with an imaginary partner. Briann's zest for life was as fiery as her gorgeous mane of red, curly hair.

Briann grabbed Rebecca's hands and forced her to dance. The two friends twirled and laughed and hugged and cried until they both collapsed onto the bed, sated and breathless. Finally Rebecca rose. "I've got to get dressed," she said, stepping into the walk-in closet that adjoined a dressing room. "It starts at seven. It's already six!"

"Wear your new skirt, like me," Briann begged. Both girls had purchased matching skirts and nearly matching blouses on one of their many shopping sprees at the Galleria.

Rebecca's lavender skirt came with a shade darker sash. A jeweled yoke crowned her white, eyelet-lace blouse. Briann's skirt and sash were two tones of red.

As she stepped into black pumps, Rebecca noticed Briann tugging outfits off of hangers, holding them to herself while peering into a full-length mirror attached to the back of the bathroom door. Her lips formed a secret smile. Other friends snubbed their noses at Rebecca's wealth, but Briann innocently delighted in it.

Unfortunately, Rebecca was deemed unapproachable by many of her classmates. Others sought her friendship as a means of getting into superior clothing shops and the finest restaurants. Rebecca believed Briann was different and felt blessed with such a friend.

After weaving her hair into a French twist, Rebecca looped two gold rings though pierced lobes and applied a touch of blush that only enhanced her natural beauty. "Let's go," she quipped to her friend.

The air seemed electrically charged as the girls bounded down the flight of stairs, disappearing into the grand crowd gathered in their honor.

Briann wandered off to merge with the crowd while Rebecca stood at the entry, greeting guests as they arrived. The two valets hired for the evening were kept on their toes as car after car poured in. Suddenly, a faded blue station-wagon that Rebecca knew all too well rolled up the cobblestone drive.

The man stepped out of the car and stumbled up the massive steps, finally greeting Rebecca under the archway.

Rebecca donned her loveliest smile and greeted the man with all the gaiety she could muster. "Hello, Uncle Kane! How nice of you to come!"

"And hello to you, shweet thing," he slurred, staggering

over the threshold.

Rebecca knew her uncle was drunk, and her stomach formed a knot. If he ruined her celebration, she would never forgive him. But she was ill prepared for what he did next.

His hands grasped her shoulders, and he plastered his face against hers, smothering her with a kiss that lasted too long for comfort.

"And how'sh the prettiest baby in the world?" He loosened his hold on her shoulders and drew her up tightly to him by fastening one arm around her waist.

"I'm fine, Uncle Kane." Exasperation edged her tone. "But I have other guests to attend to, if you don't mind."

Kane dropped his arm and stared wide-eyed, as though shocked. "Am I not a guest?" he croaked, cocking his head to one side. An oily lock of hair dangled lewdly over one eye. He had at least three days growth of beard on his face and his teeth looked sticky and yellow, his breath foul. His clothes, wrinkled and disorderly, hung from his emaciated form. "I realize the invitation must have gotten lost in the mail," he added sarcastically, leaning close to Rebecca's face. "I know you wouldn't forget your favorite uncle."

"I'm sorry you didn't get your invitation, Uncle Kane, but I'm sure one was sent. Maybe it'll be in the mailbox by tomorrow. There was probably a mixup somewhere."

Rebecca continued to greet incoming guests with a forced grin while trying to pacify her uncle at the same time. *Why didn't Kane get an invitation?* she wondered. Maria had sent them out, but Rebecca wasn't about to tell Kane that. She didn't want him messing with her nanny. He was malicious by nature and being drunk didn't improve his disposition. Kane's wrath was usually directed at her father, but lately he'd been taking it out on everyone. His jealousy over his brother's control of the family fortune caused undue stress on them all, and Rebecca was tired of it.

Now Kane glared at her. "What is it? Don't you think I'm good enough to be the uncle of a know-it-all, Yale-bound brat?"

She sucked in a breath, but let it out with relief at the sight of the next visitor who sauntered in. Pushing her way around Kane, she grasped Jimmy's hands in her own.

"Jimmy, I'm so glad you could make it!"

"You okay?" he asked her, noticing Kane's presence. Jimmy knew the problems Kane caused Rebecca's family. His drunken expeditions were easy fodder for gossips. He was a regular at the bars around Houston.

She nodded. "Fine, now that you're here."

Jimmy led her away, but not before burning a look into Kane that could have melted a glacier. "Come on, let's mingle. Others are just trickling in. It's time to enjoy yourself."

Rebecca squeezed Jimmy's hand with gratitude as they headed for the catered buffet and a night of reminiscing about days gone by and thoughts of what the future held in store.

Rebecca's mother showed up shortly after Kane, and the two spent most of the evening drinking heavily and being obnoxious.

Rebecca's father had sported her around to all his business guests, introducing her with great pleasure. All the friends she dearly loved were there and a host of relatives she hadn't seen in years. With Jimmy at her side, Rebecca had no more trouble with Kane—only an occasional, sinister glare that sent tingles rippling up her spine.

The rest of the party passed uneventfully, and it was after midnight before the last of the guests made their way home.

In the early morning hours, completely exhausted, Rebecca lay limp against the linen sheets covering her bed. She nodded off as soon as her head touched the pillow, failing to hear the heavy footsteps that stopped beside her bed. She awakened to a hand pressed tightly against her mouth. Her heart pounded until she felt it would burst from her chest.

Although Rebecca couldn't see her attacker because of the darkness, she could smell him. The scent of sweat and alcohol told her exactly who it was. Kane! She retched at the strong, repulsive smell of his breath as he whispered, "If you scream, I'll choke the air right out of you."

Rebecca knew he meant it. Her body stiffened as he slid his hand from her mouth and under the front of her nightgown. Tears rose in her eyes. She shivered uncontrollably. "Please don't. . ." she begged him. His breathing came in spurts, choppy and uneven.

"You're my uncle!" she cried, trying to reason with him. "Don't do this!"

He placed his unshaven face inches from hers. "I'm not your uncle," he told her. "I've no blood ties with you, pretty miss." Rebecca gasped in disbelief. "Didn't anybody tell you, baby? You're adopted. A throw away." More hissing laughter escaped his throat.

Rebecca flailed her fists at him and kicked with the one leg that wasn't pinned down.

He grabbed both her hands in one large hand. She tried to twist them from his grip. It was rock solid. His other hand roamed free and Rebecca felt herself losing consciousness while his words echoed inside her head like a boomerang.

four

The first thing Rebecca saw the next morning was Maria's concerned eyes. The nanny had come to wake her and found her curled up in a protective ball to ward off the terror the night had brought.

"*Enferma?*" Maria asked as she placed a cool hand against Rebecca's forehead.

Rebecca explained that she wasn't sick, but she couldn't hide the fact that something was wrong. Maria pulled the girl to a sitting position on the mussed bed.

"What is it then? You did not wake up early as usual."

Rebecca hugged herself and peered around the room as though seeing it for the first time.

"I'm just tired," she assured the servant. She wanted to scream, "My uncle raped me last night!" Yet she couldn't tell Maria about the rape. She knew her nanny would confront Kane and was afraid of what her uncle would do in response. He was out of control, and if he ever did anything to Maria, Rebecca would never forgive herself.

Maria, momentarily pacified, pointed to a silver tray loaded down with orange juice, a bowl of oatmeal, and toast—Rebecca's favorite breakfast. Next to the silverware was a thick white envelope with a beautiful Del Bar rose, fresh from the florist.

"Maybe you had to much fiesta last night, no? Eat, *niña.* It will make you feel better." Then Maria headed down the flight of stairs with the morning laundry piled in her arms.

Not hungry, Rebecca stared at the tray of food. Stretching her arms toward the nightstand, she gripped the small glass of orange juice in one hand and the envelope in the other.

The juice soothed Rebecca's parched throat. She had cried most of the night, and the emotional and physical abuse she had endured had set into her system like a bad case of pneumonia. When she looked at the red rose, it was not the delicate blossom she saw, but the thorns that adorned its long stem. It reminded her of the thorns around Jesus' head on the day of his crucifixion. She refused to touch it.

Opening the envelope, Rebecca was surprised to find five hundred dollars in cash and a check made out to her for another thousand. Then she found the folded piece of white stationary. Rebecca recognized her father's handwriting, and as she read the note, tears fell on the words, smudging the ink. But the message was still discernible.

Hi, sweetheart:

Sorry I missed you at breakfast this morning. I decided to let you sleep in. You must be exhausted after the party. I have to make a quick flight to Amarillo. Wanted to tell you that I am so proud of you. The rose is a token of my love. The cash is gas money or whatever you want to use it for. The check is something to get you started in college. And what awaits you outside your bedroom window is merely a gift from your mother and me. I love you, sweetheart, and will see you late this evening.

Love, Dad.

Dad, she mused. *Who and where is my real father?*

Rebecca placed the note under her pillow and stood. She took painful steps to the bay window and peered through its leaded glass panes. Below her second story window, parked just outside the grand entrance of the Wesbrook Estate, was a beautiful red Porsche with a white bow adorning its roof.

She would need a vehicle for college. College. A word with no meaning now.

Feeling numb, Rebecca hurried into tennis clothes and ran down to the courts for her lesson. The morning sun beat down unmercifully on her tense shoulders and neck. Sweat ran in tiny rivers down the length of her back and created jagged paths down the sides of her face, but it wasn't the May heat that bothered her.

The girl pivoted her body toward the fluffy yellow balls served her way, executing less than adequate swings. She knew Tatianna was losing patience, yet she couldn't seem to muster the drive to return her teacher's expert volleys. She wanted desperately to tell someone what Kane had done, but she didn't know how. The repercussions for speaking up outweighed those for keeping quiet.

After her uncle had left her bedroom, the rape consumed her mind. In the early morning hours, she'd showered, rubbing herself raw with a loofa and dowsing herself in the hottest water she could endure. She wanted him off of her: his repulsing scent, his touch.

The memory ended as her eyes focused on the yellow ball that suddenly stung her face and bounced off, rolling to a stop at Tatianna's feet.

"What is wrong with you?" Tatianna yelled in exasperation, bending to retrieve the ball. "You've failed to return one serve sufficiently this whole hour!"

Rebecca steadied her racket in her hand. "I'm sorry."

"*Sorry* won't win the Wichita Falls Tournament next weekend!" she scolded. "Now, I'm going to go back over to my court and you *will* return these serves."

Rebecca hazarded a glance in Tatianna's direction. "Your mother will hear of this!" her teacher promised through clenched teeth.

But Rebecca could take no more. "Then tell her if it'll make you happy!" she yelled back. "Why should I care what Candace thinks? She's not even my mother!" Rebecca spun on her heel and marched off the court.

She scurried into the house just in time to hear the phone ring. It only rang once. She hoped Maria had picked it up, but her heart told her otherwise.

Taking the stairs two at a time, Rebecca crossed the hallway and leaned breathlessly against the door to her mother's bedroom. Rebecca could tell by the coarse sound in her mother's voice that she was talking to Tatianna. Her mother used a different tone when talking to certain people and this one was reserved for her tennis instructor.

Hesitating only briefly, Rebecca ran to her room and sat down at her vanity. She removed the elastic band imprisoning her hair at the nape of her neck. It felt good to shake the thick curls free and let them rest about her shoulders. She readied herself for the impending confrontation. She could hear slipper-clad feet padding down the hall toward her room.

"What exactly do you mean?" Her mother's voice announced her presence at the door.

"What do you mean by not telling me I was adopted?"

"We just didn't think you were ready. And from your attitude right now, I would say we were right!"

Rebecca stood and squared her shoulders. "When did you think I'd be ready? I'm eighteen! Besides, how did you expect me to respond?"

Candace leaned against the door's thick jam, as though needing support. "Who told you?"

"What about how I feel?"

"What difference should it make to you? Your friends would die for what you have!"

Rebecca lifted both hands in front of her. "Wait a minute. *Money* is not the subject here. Nor is how I found out." Rebecca remembered last night. "I should have been told sooner," she managed.

"We don't see it that way," Candace retorted.

"I know for a fact my father wanted to tell me. You didn't." Rebecca scanned the clock on her nightstand and despaired that is was only noon. It would be hours before her father got home. She needed him *now.*

Candace placed a thin hand on the door knob. "I want to know if your father told you."

Rebecca's cheeks grew hot.

"Who told you?" Candace repeated.

Anger swirled like a striking serpent inside of Rebecca. "My uncle told me, that's who! Uncle Kane. He informed of the *great secret* last night after the party—while I was in bed!" Rebecca sobbed openly, her words barely audible. "He told me I was adopted while he raped me!"

five

Unexpectedly, Candace twirled on her heel and marched to the top of the stair-railing. "Maria!" she yelled, her voice husky and stern. "Maria!"

What could she possibly want with Maria? Rebecca couldn't allow Candace to bring Maria into this. "No, not Maria. We can't—"

Maria's voice sounded at the bottom of the stairs. "*Si, Senora?*"

"I want you to leave!" Candace asserted. "Take the rest of the day off." There was silence.

Finally Maria spoke. "What about dinner?"

"Go now!"

"Then," Maria hesitated. "I will see you tomorrow."

Rebecca's lips fell into a frown. *Why did Candace suddenly wish Maria to leave? After all, she lived here, didn't she?*

Candace crossed the vestibule with determined steps. She entered Rebecca's bedroom and slammed the door shut, only to lean against it heavily, as though guarding against intruders. The words that flew from Candace's mouth made Rebecca wince. "Lies!"

Eyes wide with shock, Rebecca countered, "I'm not l. . .lying."

"Oh, I believe he told you that you were adopted," Candace retorted. "And you're makin' up this story because of it!"

Rebecca drew a deep, jagged breath. She looked Candace straight in the eye. "Why don't you believe me? Do you honestly think I would make something like this up?"

"Yes!" Candace's reply smarted. "Granted, Kane had no business tellin' you about the adoption. It wasn't his place. But that's no reason to set your heart on destroyin' him."

"That's not it! You don't understand!"

"I understand everything," Candace continued. "You want attention. You have always wanted more attention than I could afford you, although Shane certainly has indulged you."

Rebecca cringed at her mother's words.

"Well, you won't get it this way! Don't you know that your father lives for his brother?" Candace paused. "Yes, they fight—don't I know it. But Shane won't stand for these accusations concernin' his brother. Neither will I."

Candace whirled around and gripped the doorknob. She opened the door a crack before glancing back at Rebecca. "There's one more thing you might want to consider before tellin' these lies to anyone else. Your father will never look at you the same, Rebecca, because you will have shamed him with your accusations. Besides," she added before turning her back on Rebecca, "if you tell anyone, nobody will believe a word you say. Trust me." With that, she disappeared.

Numbly, Rebecca stepped to the bay window and peered out. *Maybe some fresh air will help clear my mind,* she reasoned, wandering out of her room toward the library.

When she entered the large room, curtained wall to wall with books, the musty odors brought her partly out of her stupor, reviving poignant memories.

Rebecca remembered as a child sitting in the middle of the room on the colorful oriental rugs, watching slivers of sunlight dance about on the oak-paneled walls as the sun sliced through the glossy foliage of the winterberry trees in the garden. On a windy day, it was a true wonderland. But now, that awestruck innocence of her childhood had disappeared.

Rebecca meandered to the door. Opening it, she stepped quietly out onto the balcony and peered out with blurred vision toward the garden, her father's pride and joy.

A pained smile touched her trembling lips as she remembered the many walks the two of them had taken through the garden in the spring, summer, and fall. Some had been in the early morning when dew was still thick on the ground; others were in the early evening when the low sun was bordered by a curtain of lavender and fiery orange. She remembered their many heartfelt talks over full blossoms of delicate crimson, pink, and white candelabra primrose.

Rebecca realized she could never intentionally hurt her father. What if Candace were right? Could she risk it?

Her father meant the world to her, as did Maria. She could never hurt them. . .by any means. She must bear this burden alone. A shrill ring broke through her thoughts. Remembering Maria had gone for the day, Rebecca dashed back indoors to the desk. Before it could ring a second time, she lifted the phone's black receiver.

Her father's voice sounded warm and festive on the

other end. Rebecca knew he was happy.

"How's my graduate doing?" he asked gleefully.

A knot formed in Rebecca's throat. "She's doing just fine, Daddy," she managed. There was a moment's pause and Rebecca felt her father might have read something in her tone.

"Well. . .what do you think?" Shane finally quizzed.

"About what?" Rebecca was puzzled as to what he was referring to. Another pause. Suddenly she remembered and blurted out before he could answer. "Thanks so much, Daddy! It's beautiful—the car. And the rose!" she hurriedly added. "And thank you for the money, too."

"You've earned it, kiddo. I just hope you enjoy that car. Is it the right color?"

Rebecca tried to sound cheerful. "Oh, yes! I love red! You know that." Her father sounded so happy, happier than she could remember. She couldn't possibly dampen his happiness with her pain. "When will you be home?" she managed.

"I won't be home 'til around ten tomorrow. Didn't Mom tell you?"

The answer caused her heart to ache. A flood of hot tears brimmed her eyes, making them glisten like emeralds.

"I don't recall," she choked.

"I'm sorry, baby. Some unexpected business came up. But I'll take an early flight," he quickly added.

From there, Rebecca's father monopolized the conversation with details of his business trip, but all she could think about was the incident and her mother's reaction. Maybe her mother was right, although none of it made sense. Did she have the right to drop the bomb on everybody else, just because it had been dropped on her? And, what if it *did* change the way her father felt about her? She couldn't risk her father's love. The horrid, awful, unfair truth of it all engulfed her.

"Becca. Becca!" The voice tugged at her thoughts.

"I'm here, Daddy," Rebecca answered. "I'm sorry I wasn't paying attention."

"That's all right, baby. You've probably got a lot on your mind."

"I do," Rebecca said. "I'm sorry."

"Don't be," her father returned. "I understand. Just wanted to hear your voice. I can't tell you how proud I am of you, Becca."

Rebecca wanted to feel his tender arms around her, holding her, keeping her safe. "Thanks, Daddy."

"I'll see you tomorrow morning and we can have a long talk then, maybe a nice walk in the garden."

"Uh huh," was all she could offer, her voice trembling as much as her bottom lip.

"Bye, honey. Sleep tight and I'll see you in the morning."

Rebecca cleared her throat. "Okay," she mustered.

"I love you."

"I love you too, Daddy."

Click.

Holding the receiver tightly against her chest, Rebecca allowed the tears to fall freely. It was then she heard the other click.

She burst from the library and dashed down the hall straight toward Candace's closed bedroom door. She grasped the knob on the door and flung it open. "How dare you!" she screamed. "How dare you listen in on my conversations! You have no right!"

Candace stood from her sitting position on the bed, the phone's receiver still warm in its cradle. Her voice was cool and indignant. "Of course I have a right, darlin'. This is my house; you are my daughter."

"You're right, you know," Rebecca pointed out. "This *is* your house—"

"I'm glad we agree," Candace interrupted.

"But I am *not* your daughter!" Rebecca countered. With that, she turned and strode from the room.

It was 3:00 P.M. when Rebecca finished cramming the rest of her belongings in the last suitcase. She gripped them both by their tortoise shell handles. She couldn't take everything, so she seized only what she deemed necessary: Her best clothes, makeup, and toiletries. She didn't forget to stuff the fat envelope of bills, the check, and the note into her black leather clutch. "God help me," she whispered under her breath. Then she turned her back on the Wesbrook Estate.

Clouds clumped abundantly in the azure sky above her as Rebecca climbed behind the wheel of the red Porsche. She let out a relieved breath when she saw the keys in the ignition.

White leather squeaked beneath her as she started the engine and placed a foot on the gas peddle. She had no idea where she was going, but she couldn't stay in her childhood home any longer. She wanted to go where nobody could find her.

The car rolled down the circular drive smoothly, effortlessly, as Rebecca pondered her options. The sun's warm evening rays glanced off the shiny red paint of the car as she headed for the interstate.

She couldn't show up at college, she realized. They would find her and discover her terrible secret. Shame engulfed her. Heat surfaced in her cheeks. Although it wasn't her fault, she would be blamed.

"It's not fair!" She screamed the words, but all she could hear was her own labored breathing and the soft hum of the tires on the smooth pavement.

six

As Rebecca left the exclusive development she had always called home, hot tears stung her eyes. Where could she go? For hours, she kept driving. The panic of loneliness set in. She thought of Briann, but remembered her friend had left on a family vacation that morning.

Suddenly, a different panic set in. What would Candace—she could never call that woman her mother again—tell her father when he returned from Amarillo? Maybe, if she had time to explain things to him, he would understand.

Rebecca punched the gas pedal with her foot and sped toward I-45. "God," she whispered, "help me reach him before Candace does."

Before long, she was heading north with enough gas to get to Dallas. Her father had filled the tank before giving her the car.

Soon, she was in the midst of Huntsville, not a big town. She pulled into the first convenient store parking lot she came to, purchased a cup of coffee, and visited the restroom before heading down the road again.

As she sipped the scalding liquid, she hoped it would revive her enough so that she could make it to Dallas before stopping for the night. She couldn't help the feelings of betrayal that riveted through her consciousness. She knew Candace was capable of many things. But, not this.

The green neon of the car's glowing digital clock read 9:00 as Rebecca approached the Dallas city limits. Colorful, gleaming signs adorned the freeway telling travellers of the best eateries and motels. Dallas's skyline illuminated the dark sky and a throbbing moon hung awkwardly alone above the skyscrapers.

Rebecca took the next exit. She was exhausted and had to keep the radio blaring to stay awake. Soon she'd have a bed to curl up in, but first her car needed gas. The gauge read just above empty. She was in luck. A gas station was on the other side of the overpass with a motel one more block down the street.

Rebecca maneuvered the Porsche in as close beside the self-service pump as she could. She opened the door, stood, and stretched her body toward the black sky. Then she set about the task of pumping gas. She squeezed the handle after inserting the nozzle in the opening to her car's tank. Nothing came out. After working the handle several more times, still nothing happened.

An old, beat up Chevy pick-up pulled up on the other side of her pump. She studied the old man while pretending to pump the gas. He removed the nozzle, which she had done, then flipped the latch that it rested on upward before inserting the nozzle.

"Ah!" she said out loud. The old man didn't seem to notice. Maybe he was hard of hearing.

Flipping the latch up, the gas flowed freely and Rebecca grew more at ease. She had never pumped her own gas before, but the new independence felt good.

After she paid for the gas, Rebecca snuggled back into her seat and started the engine. She shifted into reverse, and the car rolled backward. Before she could peer into the rearview mirror, she heard an awful scraping sound. The red Porsche jolted and came to a complete stop.

Rebecca felt like a tornado settled in her stomach as she shifted back into park and stepped out of the car. Her gaze met with beautiful sky-blue eyes, belonging to a man seated at the wheel of a black Mercedes.

His hair was as black as his car and wavy, making his blue eyes stand out like sapphires against black velvet.

He opened his door slowly and swung long legs out onto the pavement. He was tall and Rebecca could easily see he was fit, even under the expensive gray suit he wore.

His white shirt, open at the throat, exposed a thick neck. A tie had been thrown across the passenger seat beside him. *He must be returning from, not going somewhere,* thought Rebecca.

The accident was her own fault, she reasoned, watching him approach the rear of her car, obviously to inspect the damage.

The man seemed to wait for Rebecca to make the first move. His steely gaze made her blush.

"I'm very sorry," she said. The man drew his gaze from her and surveyed the damage to the front of his car, ignoring her apology.

"It doesn't look too bad to me. Just a fender scratch."

Rebecca's breath seemed to even out as relief flooded her nerves. "I'm sorry," she repeated, grateful he seemed a man with a forgiving nature. "I've been driving all night and just didn't think to look behind me. I hope its repairable."

"Who do you have insurance with?"

Insurance! She had never given that a thought. *Surely*

Daddy had purchased insurance when he purchased the vehicle.

She raked a slender hand through her auburn curls as though the act would help her think better. "I'm not certain I have insurance," she offered sheepishly. The man did not look amused."But I have cash with me," she added hurriedly. "I can pay for the damage now if you like." It wasn't a deep scratch, and Rebecca felt certain she would have enough to cover it.

A dark curl dipped slightly over one eye as the man tilted his head toward the ground, thinking intently. Rebecca chewed on her bottom lip.

"I don't know how much the repairs will run," said the stranger. "I'm not a mechanic. I'm a lawyer."

Rebecca winced at his remark. Her heart pounded in her chest until she felt it would burst. Of all the people to hit, it would have to be a lawyer—even a forgiving one.

"Why don't you leave me your name and a number I can reach you at when I get back to town?" he finally offered.

Rebecca noticed he now looked at her with the same intent gaze he had just used while studying the damage to his car. She nearly ripped her leather clutch open as she fumbled for paper and something to write with. Then she saw the pen in his grip not two inches from her face. His brown leather briefcase lay open on the hood of the Mercedes and he calmly withdrew a sheet of yellow legal paper.

Anger swept through her. It was simply an accident and he didn't need to behave so arrogantly! She tore the paper and pen from his grip and was dismayed to see it had little impact on his attitude. He looked as cold as a frost-covered pine.

She had just written her first name when it dawned on her. How could she put her real name down? And what telephone number would she use? She didn't want to leave any clues about who she was.

Clearing her throat, Rebecca wrote a false last name: *Wood.* It would have to do. The only thing that came to mind quickly was her home in the Woodlands. And a number? She would have to make that up also.

Handing the paper and pen back to the stranger, Rebecca took a deep breath, hoping he wouldn't elaborate. She watched him as he studied the information.

"Rebecca?" he asked. "Your name is Rebecca Wood?"

"Yes," she replied curtly, feeling guilty for not being truthful. Her Christian upbringing rallied against the lie, but she forced herself to ignore her conscience. If anyone found her, she would never reach her father before Candace did. Maybe Candace had the police after her right now!

"And this area code. It's Dallas, right?"

"Right," she said quickly, hoping she sounded convincing. It *was* a Dallas area code. She had seen it many times on the billboards she had passed coming into the city. The number belonged to one of the motels along the strip.

As Rebecca straightened her things inside her purse, he handed her a card. His business card. Without looking at it, she stuffed it into the bottom of her clutch. She vowed to herself that when she was able she would make things right with the man.

The stranger seemed satisfied and paper-clipped the

note to the top sheet of a pile of documents inside the briefcase before snapping it shut.

"I'll be getting in touch," he said with a slight wave.

Exhausted, Rebecca merely nodded and retreated to the quiet of her car. She desperately needed a bed.

Checking the view beside, in front of, and in back of her car, Rebecca finally released the brake. She wasn't taking any chances this time and headed down the strip bulging with motels, restaurants, and billboard signs.

After signing in at the nearest Howard Johnson's, Rebecca wove her way up the steps. The room's contemporary decor and squeaky clean smell went unnoticed as she dropped her bags and flung herself across the width of the queen-size bed.

seven

Groggy and disoriented, Rebecca drug herself out of bed. Her watch read one in the morning. It was only then she realized she hadn't received the midnight wake-up call she'd asked for. Or was she so exhausted that she simply didn't hear it?

Without so much as brushing her teeth, she grabbed her belongings and dashed from the motel. Her heart pounded, believing she might not catch up to her father before he left Amarillo. She needed desperately to get on the road if she was to reach him before he left his office and boarded the morning flight back to Houston. He was her last hope.

Sipping the cup of scalding coffee between bites of a cinnamon roll she had purchased at a convenience store, Rebecca studied the barrage of green signs overhead and to the right of her until she found I-287 north out of Dallas. She had a full tank of gas and all the car indicators seemed all right. Still, as she reached the interstate and accelerated, Rebecca said a silent prayer.

For a brief second her faith left her and fear settled in the pit of her stomach. Was God really with her? Or was she alone on the Staked Plains of Texas? She shuddered visibly and focused on the long stretch of highway in front of her.

A glowing moon lent a halo of light to the countryside, revealing an abrupt change in landscape. Trees became sparse, cactus and blue yucca plentiful. Soon she witnessed the blend of Indian paintbrush reds mingled with golden-beard penstemon. The plains were purified by the delicate whites of sweet clover and the creamy, pastel pinks of the bindweed. In the distance, she caught movement and realized a herd of antelope grazed placidly there on the abundant bunch grass. The sight of them brought her a fleeting feeling of serenity. God was with her. All around her.

In Childress, she grabbed a burger and quickly filled her tank with gas. She had to keep moving if she was to reach her father in time. There was nothing between towns except endless horizon and, at times, breathtaking scenery.

Soon she was through Clarendon and the little green signs read Amarillo along with several other smaller towns. Rebecca breathed a sigh of relief. She was almost there!

Just out of Washburn, she took I-40 and entered the city of Amarillo. A glance at the dashboard clock revealed 7:15. Pulling off onto the shoulder of the road, Rebecca snatched a crumpled piece of paper from her clutch. The address she had taken from her father's address book said FISS was located on Georgia. Opening the paper on the seat beside her, she resumed driving. The Georgia exit led her through the heart of the city, forcing her to stop every few seconds for a light. Enough time to scan the buildings for the name of her father's company.

A smile touched her still lips when she saw the bold lettering *FISS* on the face of a tall, white stone building with mirrored glass glistening at every window and door, very modern architecture.

When she pulled into the parking lot reserved for FISS employees across the street from the business itself, she couldn't contain the joy that made her heart leap in her chest. A tawny sun bathing the city in its new light only enhanced this.

She couldn't wait to peer into her father's eyes, security in the hostile world. Rebecca nearly ran up the sparkling granite steps leading to mirrored glass doors. To her dismay, she couldn't budge them.

As she tugged and tugged on the brass handle her frown returned. She began knocking furiously. *Where's Dad?*

She remembered that he always came in early on the mornings he flew back to Houston to double-check last minute details. He should be there!

Pounding furiously on the glass, she grew furious that she could not see into the building. The only thing she saw was her reflection: a pale, drawn face framed by a shock of auburn curls that flailed about in a sudden gust of wind. Her jeans and T-shirt looked rumpled and disorderly. It had never occurred to her to change after sleeping in them. Now she wished she had.

Just when her expectations were crushed, Rebecca heard the clacking approach of a woman's low-heeled shoes. She drew a deep breath and moved a few inches away from the door. The woman who greeted her was mature with hair drawn into a widow's bun at the nape of her neck and flecked with gray. The tortoise-shell-framed glasses she wore appeared too large for her face. She scanned Rebecca through their glass prisms from head to toe.

"Can I help you?"

Rebecca clasped her fingers around her flying auburn locks and held it like a rubber band at the nape of her neck to keep it out of her face. "Yes," she said in as professional a tone as she could muster. "I'm Rebecca W. . .Wood." *Forgive me God,* she said to herself. Not until she saw her father would she drop her defenses. The new name was as comforting to her as a security blanket to a frightened child.

"I would like to see Mr. Shane Wesbrook if I may."

Opening the door, the woman asked, "Mr. Wesbrook of FISS?"

"Yes." Rebecca was relieved when the woman allowed her entry and ushered her through a long marble corridor with executive suites down both sides.

Led into a room with glossy textured walls and an ultra-modern design reflecting tones of peach, rust, and gray, she was seated in a light peach chair. The woman extended a wrinkled hand to which Rebecca extended her own. Their fingers touched briefly, like soft-winged butterflies. "I'm Grace Southerland."

Placing her glasses low on the bridge of her nose, the woman peered at Rebecca.

"Do you have an early appointment with Mr. Wesbrook?" the woman asked as she removed her glasses and held them clasped precariously between a stubby index finger and thumb.

"No, ma'am," Rebecca intoned, moistening her lips with her tongue, "but I was told I could reach him here."

The clustered set of lines above the woman's raised eyebrows told Rebecca she was not trusted. Maybe it was her apparel or her youth, she wasn't sure, but she grew tired of the interrogation that made her feel like a criminal.

Rebecca took a deep breath, allowing her chest to rise and fall in plain view so the woman could see her agitation. "Look," she asserted, "I simply want to see Mr. Wesbrook. Now, *is* he in or *isn't* he?"

She locked gazes with the woman for what seemed an eternity. Finally, the woman spoke, her tone harsh.

"Mr. Wesbrook isn't in."

Rebecca's heart sank. Surely he hadn't already come and gone. "When did he leave?" Rebecca's lips tightened in disappointment. Her dark brows dug into the creamy beginnings of her nose.

"Obviously you have had some doings with Mr. Wesbrook," the woman suggested. "All I can tell you is that he got a call from his wife about some family emergency." With that, the woman marched to the door from which she came and disappeared through it.

The knot that formed in Rebecca's throat nearly gagged her, causing tears to squeeze from her reddened eyes. She plopped her weary body back into the previously occupied chair and buried her head in her hands. Tears flowed freely and her body heaved with choked breaths as she sobbed silently.

Candace had won. The trip, all of it, was useless. What had Candace told her father, and what did he think of her now? Shame engulfed her.

Wiping at her eyes, Rebecca rose and wandered slowly back down the hall. The last suite's door was open and Rebecca noticed the same woman peering at her from a large, polished desk, probably making sure she found her way out of the building.

She strained against the glass door, fighting the wind that had gained in strength since her arrival. Her hair whipped about her face as she made her way to the parking lot.

Rebecca plunged her key into the car lock and dropped like a bag of bolts into the leather seat. The engine hummed as she piloted the car onto the boulevard and began searching for a hotel. She must find someplace safe. And as she pulled into the hotel's lot, located just off I-40 and Georgia, Rebecca knew she must never look back. A vow to find out who she really was, who her real parents were, became her only strength.

eight

After a hot shower, Rebecca dressed in a khaki skirt and blouse. Her only jewelry was a pair of genuine pearl earrings pressed into her pierced lobes. Job-hunting was not an easy task, and she would need to look her best. Although she still had much of her cash and all of her check, she knew it wouldn't last forever.

Examining the classified ads in the complimentary newspaper left at her door by the hotel staff, Rebecca noticed a listing for a position at the law firm, Trevor Houston and Associates. Rebecca believed she fit the requirements perfectly, having taken business electives in high school. She could file, type, and write shorthand, all of which were required for the job. Yet, she did find it ironic that the place she was escaping from and the job she was applying for had the same name: Houston.

Drawing a pen from her purse, she scribbled the name and address on an Amarillo map. Although she would probably lose her scholarship, she would at least be working in the area of her chosen field: law. Right now her main concern was survival.

Traffic was slow, giving her time to glance at the map several times.

Finally, she pulled into a parking lot in the reserved customer section. She peered into the rearview mirror and faked a smile. Perfect white teeth gleamed back at her. Plum colored lipstick outlined well-shaped lips, and a light application of blush only enhanced the depths of her green eyes. Her tumble of auburn curls was clean and in place. She was ready.

Upon entering the building, the smells and sounds of professionalism added to her agitation. Her breathing grew choppy.

Computers raced and people milled about. Tellers greeted lines of customers at a long marble desk that ran the length of the east wall. Rebecca took her place in the shortest line and bit on her bottom lip as she waited.

When her turn finally came, she was greeted with a warm smile. "May I help you?"

For a moment Rebecca went blank, but recovered quickly. She had never been this nervous before. Not even at her graduation. Twisting a lock of hair around her index finger, Rebecca murmured, "I. . .I need to find suite 1200, please."

"Right through those glass doors." The woman pointed toward atrium doors that led to a long corridor, obviously adorned with suites. "Last door on the left."

Rebecca offered a meek, "Thank you," before walking self-consciously toward the doors. She studied her posture, making a conscious effort not to slump.

When she approached the suite, she didn't have to search for the number. She recognized the title as the same in the ad: Trevor Houston and Associates. Rebecca blew out a charged breath and gripped the doorknob.

A woman with bobbed, light brown hair kept her back to Rebecca as she punched keys on a computer keyboard, while obviously studying a garble of green words on the computer screen. Rebecca took a seat at one of the two chairs across from the desk. As she waited, she drank in the surroundings.

The blues and rusts underlying the Southwest style created a peaceful atmosphere. Trail paintings adorned the walls and an Indian prayer on parchment stood out on the wall to her right, next to another door. A framed copy of the Lord's Prayer hung beside it. An authentic looking Native American shield and an Alibates flint arrowhead collection hung just to one side of the two prayers.

Rebecca studied the back of the woman's head. When she saw no acknowledgement to her presence, she turned back to the prayer and mimed the words with her lips, the only thing familiar in her world at the moment.

"Our Father, who art in heaven. . ."

Whoever Trevor Houston was, he must be interested in the Christian faith to have made this choice of wall decoration. Rebecca had no time to mull over the prospect. The woman across from her wheeled around in her chair. "May I help you?" she asked.

Rebecca was warmed by the smile that caressed ample lips.

She smiled back, feeling more at ease. Her last experience with office personnel had left her anxious. "Yes," she managed. "I'm applying for the job you advertised in the paper."

The sparkle in the woman's sea-blue eyes that gazed out from rotund features didn't go unnoticed by Rebecca.

"Yes!" the woman said, extending a hand with puffy fingers for Rebecca to grasp. "I'm Heather Houston. I'll get you an application."

Rebecca relaxed in her seat. *Must be a father-daughter team,* she mused. She liked the family atmosphere. And the woman's warm nature helped her to calm down. She couldn't help but like Heather as she watched her strain to bend and open a file drawer to her left. She retrieved a long, white information sheet and Rebecca felt her shoulders hunch. This could take forever!

"Fill this out," Heather said as she attached the sheet to an empty clipboard. She hunted a pen from a plastic holder on the cluttered oak desk in front of her until she found one with black ink and handed it to Rebecca.

"Thank you," Rebecca offered hesitantly, glancing over the questions down the front. Most of them asked for basic information such as name and address. Others asked for credentials. Her heart weighed as heavy as a ship's anchor. The woman in front of her seemed to notice.

"Is there something you need help with?"

Shifting in her seat, Rebecca explained, "I just moved to town."

"That's no problem," the woman assured almost before Rebecca could finish her sentence. Her words took the edge off Rebecca's anxiety. "Just fill out what you can."

"I'm in a hotel right now," said Rebecca. "Can I use that as my address?"

"Absolutely!"

Confidently, Rebecca offered more. "I don't have credentials, and I just graduated."

"How old are you?"

Rebecca faltered. She didn't want everything to be a lie. Her name would be enough and even that was too much. "I'm eighteen." Rebecca's eyes widened with anticipation at Heather's long pause, nearly shattering her newfound confidence.

Heather eyed her quizzically. "You certainly had *me* fooled." She smiled warmly again. "I thought you were much older."

"That's not a problem?" Rebecca asked as she wrote in her alias and the hotel she was staying at.

The woman laughed openly and waved a fleshy hand in the air as though swatting at an imaginary fly. "Not if you can do the job!"

The woman's exuberant nature rubbed off on Rebecca. There was nothing fake in her spirited blue eyes. Insincerity was an annoying trait. This woman was true in identity and had a way of putting someone at ease.

Rebecca filled in the information to the best of her ability, leaving some blanks empty. Though she didn't have experience, she did have her skills to list. She gave her previous address as Houston, but put no street address. Her social security number was given correctly. The only inaccurate information was her name.

When she completed all she could, Rebecca handed the clipboard and pen back to Heather who perused them briefly.

"Great!" Heather said. "I'll be right back."

When Heather stood, Rebecca's eyebrows lifted skyward. No wonder the woman was pudgy. She was pregnant!

Clearing her throat, Rebecca asked, "How long?"

"'Bout a month," Heather answered, rubbing her belly affectionately with her free hand while holding the clipboard and application in the other. "If you're hired, you'll be taking my place," she laughed. "I'll be right back," she added before disappearing through the second door Rebecca had noticed earlier.

When she returned, her hands were empty. "All set," she said as Rebecca stood. "I put them on Mr. Houston's desk and he'll let me know when he can schedule an interview. He prefers to do them himself," she added with a hunch of her shoulders.

Rebecca extended a gracious hand. "Thank you so much."

Heather gripped Rebecca's slender fingers and smiled. "We can reach you at the hotel?"

The corners of Rebecca's mouth tilted down as she wondered how long she could use the hotel as home base. "Yes," she finally answered. "My room is 143, but if I find a place before you call, I'll get back to you."

Heather dropped to her chair as though the load of the baby was too much for her to bear for long periods of time. "Good luck," she offered breathlessly.

"Thanks," said Rebecca, gripping the doorknob. "And good luck to you," she added before breezing through the door and closing it softly behind her.

Back at the hotel, Rebecca perused through the newspaper again. She wanted to find someplace that was stable, an apartment or something. Hotels were not cheap.

She ran a nail down the furnished apartment section under rentals when her eyes caught on something of interest. Glendale Manor Apartments on Paramount had one-, two-, and three-bedroom units for varying rates.

Rebecca needed a two-bedroom; a room to sleep and one to study in when she started night school. She would have to give a small deposit and first month's rent. When she dialed the number, the man on the other end offered to show her an apartment at her earliest convenience.

"How about thirty minutes from now?" Rebecca asked.

It was already noon. "Oh, and it will need to be unfurnished." The furnished rates were beyond her current budget.

It was set. Rebecca gathered her black clutch and raced to her car. One thing she would have to do immediately was cash the check her father had given her for a thousand dollars. That was easily taken care of at a check cashing booth and only cost her ten dollars.

Her leather-banded quartz watch confirmed she had ten minutes to spare when she pulled up to one of several large brick apartment sections. The sign on the door read *Manager* and Rebecca rapped on the solid wood door gently with her knuckles.

A stocky, balding man of about fifty years greeted her. He spoke with such sluggishness that Rebecca had to stifle her concern.

As they made their way up a set of steps, one set of many in the complex, she was aware of his labored breathing. Even when they were indoors, his rasping breaths did not abate. But he certainly seemed unaffected by it as he droned on with the details of the apartments and why they were better than the rest, convenience being a plus as the complex was within walking distance of a mall.

After showing Rebecca around, he stuck his thumbs in his belt loops on jeans that drooped just below his paunchy stomach. "We pay water," he offered, flashing a set of teeth that were obviously false. They were too perfect to belong to a man of his age and declining health. But Rebecca sensed no threat from him.

She wet her lips with her tongue. "May I have another look around?"

The man sauntered to the door with an uneven gait. "I'll leave you alone," he offered, opening the door and stepping out onto the landing. "If ya decide ya want it, just drop back by the office."

"When can I move in?" she asked as she scanned a beckoning brick fireplace against the north wall of a large living area.

"It's empty and it's clean," he boasted proudly. "Choice is yours." He moved halfway down the steps before hollering, "Lock 'er up when yer done!"

Rebecca ran a hand over smooth ivory walls as she made her way down the hall.

The bath was small, but more than adequate for her, as were the two bedrooms. She delighted in the open bar that separated the kitchen from the living area, creating a spacious atmosphere that was enhanced by ivory walls and plush almond carpet.

After weighing the price, location, and tasteful decor, inside and out, Rebecca trotted down the steps and returned to the main office. She handed the man the cash and signed a six-month lease to his obvious glee.

"Welcome to Glendale!" he spouted as he wrote out a receipt. He walked Rebecca to her car and waited for her to start her engine before lumbering back to the office.

Pulling into a McDonald's after checking out of her motel, Rebecca grabbed a salad and soft drink. Lunch passed and she had almost forgotten to eat. She needed sustenance to keep up her strength.

She ate in one of the restaurant's many booths and felt stronger than she had in days, relieved to have found a place so quickly. Small blessings counted in a world that had turned upside down. At least she had a month to hunt for work before they could kick her out. Until then, she would have to monitor her money carefully. The thought of a job made her remember about the one she had just applied for. She would need to give them her new address.

Rebecca downed the last of her soda and drew the law firm's ad out of her purse. She made her way to a pay phone, punched a sequence of numbers, and immediately recognized the pleasant voice on the line as Heather's.

"Trevor Houston and Associates."

"Heather?"

"This is Heather."

Rebecca shuffled her feet. "This is Rebecca, Rebecca Wood. Do you re—?"

"Yes!" Heather interjected before Rebecca could finish. "I just tried to call you. They said you'd already checked out."

Clearing her throat, Rebecca added, "That's why I'm calling. I found an apartment. I needed to give you the address." Anticipation and hope filled her. She could think of only one reason Heather would call, especially so soon after their meeting. "Did you need something?"

"Yes," Heather answered. "Can you swing by the office at two o'clock?"

Rebecca stood erect. "Certainly," she replied, trying to maintain her excitement.

"Great! Mr. Houston wants to interview you. So we'll see you at two."

An interview this quickly! Could she possibly find a home and a job, all in the same day? But then, she reasoned, this is just an interview and that's all. It doesn't mean a job. Nonetheless, she slammed into the restaurant's bathroom to freshen her make-up, brush her wayward auburn locks, and smooth any wrinkles from her outfit.

When she arrived at the law firm, she was greeted with the same friendly demeanor as before. Heather looked tired as she sipped on ice water.

"Doctor says it'll help the swelling in my ankles," Heather offered to Rebecca's questioning gaze.

Just then a male voice came over the intercom. Rebecca didn't quite know why she jumped at the voice, but her heart somersaulted in her chest.

"Send Ms. Wood in."

Gripping the door knob, Rebecca turned it and pushed the door open. Her eyes widened in horror at what awaited her.

The employer on the other side of the monstrous desk glared at her with familiar blue eyes while a mocking grin tugged at his lips. Rebecca felt herself swoon as she recognized the driver of the black Mercedes, Trevor Houston, the man she had hit that early morning at the gas pump in Dallas.

nine

"So, Ms. Wood, we meet again." His tone was mocking and Rebecca couldn't gather her senses quickly enough to offer a rebuttal. She nearly dropped into one of two black leather chairs opposite the lawyer's desk.

"Are. . .are you Trevor Houston?" she finally managed, avoiding his blistering gaze. She secretly berated herself for the obvious mess she was in. But how was she supposed to know? The accident happened in Dallas. How could she possibly have known he lived in Amarillo.

"Listen," she blurted, "I told you I would pay for the damage to your car—"

He interrupted her. "And how did you intend to do that? You gave me a phony phone number."

Rebecca's face grew hot. "I realize what that must have looked like, but you don't understand—"

"Obviously not," Trevor interjected before she could finish. "Why don't you try explaining it to me?"

"It's not that easy," Rebecca mumbled. She felt helpless. "How much will the repair cost?" she finally asked, not knowing what else to say.

She watched Trevor retrieve a white sheet from underneath a stack of other business papers. "Here it is," he said, handing it across the desk to Rebecca.

She examined a list of repairs with their costs beside them. When she reached the bottom of the page, her eyes widened in horror. "Twelve hundred and thirty-eight dollars!"

"That's right." The grin left his face.

"It was only a scratch!"

"A scratch to a Mercedes can be very costly, Ms. Wood. And that's the lowest bid, for your information."

Rebecca felt the sting of his words. The estimate was legitimate and he *was* a lawyer. His surroundings told her he was a man of conscience and Christian values. A Bible sat in plain view on his desk and a plaque holding the ten commandments rested on the wall behind him. It probably *was* the lowest bid. What chance did she possibly have of winning this argument?

"I told you I'd pay for it," she intoned, "and I will!" Rebecca stood and smoothed her khaki skirt. But his next words made her stiffen.

"When can you start?"

Was he adding insult to injury? Rebecca ignored the remark and spun on her heel to face the door. She grasped the doorknob in a grip that would have popped a tennis ball. But Trevor wasn't finished.

"I asked you a question, Ms. Wood, and would like the courtesy of a reply—or are you as clumsy at decision-making as you are at driving?"

Flinging herself around to face him, she said in a quiet, angry voice, "I wouldn't work for you, *Mr. Houston,* if you were the last man on earth."

"I don't see as you have much choice."

"And just what does that mean?"

"It means you can work for me to pay off the damages to my car, or I'll be forced to turn you in to the authorities for failure to provide proof of insurance or proper

I.D., Ms. Wood."

Stunned, Rebecca could only glare. She wouldn't bother asking what the pay rate would be. Her options were limited since she obviously had no choice but to work for him.

Trevor continued, "As soon as you pay the damages in their entirety, you're welcome to locate other work. Until you do, you may work for me." He pushed a button on his intercom.

"Yes?" Heather's spirited voice came over the intercom.

"I want you to show Ms. Wood around and begin her training. She's been hired for the job."

Heather shrieked on the other end. "Does she start now?"

"Right now," Trevor answered before lifting his finger from the button. Then he stood and stepped around the desk until he was within inches of Rebecca. "Let me help you," he offered, stretching his hand for the door knob.

Was there a hint of compassion in his tone? Surely not, Rebecca thought as she stepped over the threshold. This man was incapable of empathy!

Sinking down into the chair Heather had set up beside her own, Rebecca struggled to maintain her composure, but Heather immediately sensed something was amiss.

"Are you okay?" she asked, sympathy flooding her voice.

Rebecca sat upright, drew composure from a deep breath, and smiled. She didn't want Heather to know anything about what had just transpired. "Of course," she answered. She hoped Heather wouldn't catch on. "I guess I'm just so shocked to have gotten a job so quickly."

"It's just wonderful how things turn out," offered Heather with natural optimism lacing every word. "God takes care of us."

All Rebecca could do was nod.

"Let's get started." Heather pulled papers out of several gray file cabinets and entire folders and books from locked desk drawers. She piled them up on the desk in front of them.

Heather spent the next two hours showing Rebecca where everything went: pens, pads, extra memos, and anything that needed filing. Rebecca learned how to answer the phone and pencil appointments into the schedule book.

"Mr. Houston pencils in the times he'll be in court, which is usually mornings. We generally schedule depositions and appointments with individual clients for the afternoons." Then Heather held up two form letters.

"These are our most popular," she joked. Even Rebecca smiled. "One is sent out to clients to let them know how their cases are progressing. We just fill in the blanks. If Mr. Houston needs more information, he'll call you in for dictation."

At that Rebecca bristled. The less she had to see of Trevor Houston, the better. Heather proceeded.

"The other is a suit letter sent out to parties to inform them of the suit being filed against them . . . and I almost forgot." Heather retrieved another form letter from the file box beside her. "Ths one's for collections." She paused. "Sometimes people don't pay their bills."

Rebecca scanned the letter's contents. For the most part she was eager to learn. But her heart had been so set on attending Yale. Just then the intercom on Heather's desk buzzed. A tingle shot up Rebecca's spine. It could be only one person.

"Yes?" Heather answered.

"I need you to send in Ms. Wood, that is if you're finished with her."

Heather winked at Rebecca, having no knowledge of the knot forming in the young woman's throat. "Well, I was just getting to accounts, but I suppose I can spare her for a few minutes."

Rebecca stood and raked a trembling hand through her long hair. Why did he have this impact on her? She had never been intimidated in her life, except by Candace maybe, but that was different. Grudgingly, she forced herself to open the door and face him again.

"Have a seat," said Trevor.

Rebecca dropped slowly into the same chair she had occupied earlier. Trevor's tone didn't seem as daunting as before. But she still refused to let down her guard. She pulled her shoulders back, folded her slender hands in her lap, and waited.

Trevor leaned back in his chair, making the black leather squeak with the motion. "There are some things I need to clarify with you before you go home."

Rebecca cast her gaze to a wooden chime clock on the north wall. It showed 4:45. Heather had said that quitting time was at five. Rebecca was relieved to know she had only fifteen more minutes to endure this man, for today anyhow. Tomorrow would have to take care of itself.

Trevor cleared his throat. Their gazes met and held. "I'm sure Heather has gone over as much as she could in three hours, but there are some things you should know." He paused for effect. "This is a law office, Ms. Wood, a place where confidential information is processed. My clients come to me in confidence and we will not let them down. In other words, nothing that passes in front of your eyes or through your ears is to leave your mouth. Nothing leaves this office. Understood?"

Rebecca had never been one to gossip anyhow. But Trevor didn't know that and he had every right to mistrust her, considering the circumstances. She found herself wanting him to trust her.

"Mr. Houston, you won't have to worry about that. I won't compromise the privacy of your clients. What is between us has nothing to do with them."

Trevor, apparently satisfied, leaned forward and folded his hands on the desk in front of him. "There's one more thing," he said arching one black eyebrow. "As far as your paychecks are concerned, I just wanted to give you an option."

Rebecca's body tensed.

"You have two choices," he continued. "I'm paying you $8.25 an hour starting wages on a guaranteed forty-hour week. I pay every two weeks. Now, I can take all of your first check and a portion of your second which will get you out of here in a month's time."

Mischief gleamed from his eyes and Rebecca drew a deep breath to abate the anger that swelled inside her. She maintained his gaze with her own to show him she wasn't afraid of him, although in some odd way she was. After a brief pause, he continued.

"Or I can take a small portion out of each check which would leave some for your living expenses, but it would mean you'd be here longer. The choice is yours, Ms. Wood."

"Take a little out of each paycheck," she blurted as she stood and strode to the door, pausing only to open it before she left his office and slammed the door behind her.

ten

After Trevor gleaned his share from her first paycheck, Rebecca had just enough left to pay utilities, buy groceries, and purchase a sofa and matching love seat. She saved a portion of the cash remaining from what her father had given her for the rent and filled her car's gas tank. She stuffed two twenties and a ten into her wallet for extras and put the remaining two hundred into her bank account.

Little by little, with God's help, Rebecca was building a life for herself. Although her job would be gone soon, she was secure in the knowledge that she could find another without any problem. With this job, she was gaining valuable experience and was learning the mechanics of how a well-organized law office ran. She secretly reveled in thoughts of running her own law office someday.

Enjoying the moment, Rebecca slumped onto her mauve sofa and luxuriated in its velvety softness, so soothing to her body after spending two weeks sleeping on the floor with borrowed sheets and blankets from Heather. She kicked off her shoes and contemplated the last two weeks.

She hadn't seen much of Trevor, for which she was grateful. He'd spent a week in Dallas at a lawyer's convention. This last week, he was in court. When they did see each other, neither said more than necessary to conduct business.

Rebecca's and Heather's relationship quickly went from casual acquaintances to a budding friendship. Rebecca had grown to care for Heather and the baby she carried, but marveled at how different she was from her brother. The only tenderness she saw from Trevor Houston was in Heather's company.

"He dotes over me," Heather had explained. "Especially since my husband passed away."

The news startled Rebecca. "You're a widow?"

Heather lovingly rubbed her tummy as she cooed something to the unborn baby before turning her attention back to Rebecca. "It's just me and this baby," she confided. "And Trevor," she added. "We had only been married a month when my husband died of complications due to his diabetes. It was quite unexpected."

Tears misted Rebecca's green eyes. "I. . .I'm sorry," Rebecca stammered, not knowing what else to say.

"Don't be," Heather cautioned. "Trevor's brother and I only had a short time together, but we made each moment count."

"You mean you're not Trevor's sister?"

"His sister-in-law. But Trevor refuses to tack on the in-law."

It was what Heather said next that really puzzled her.

"I was terribly sick at the time and I had no job." Heather's tone lowered almost to a whisper. Grief punctuated every word. "I had skills but no job."

"Were you sick from the pregnancy?" Rebecca had heard that some women get sick when pregnant, while others feel better than they've ever felt. It made her think of Candace, but she quickly dispelled the thought. Thinking about the past made her anxious.

Heather nodded and smoothed a short lock of hair behind her ear. "Yes," she answered, her blue eyes misting over again, "and sick with grief, too."

"Maybe I should just hush," Rebecca offered, knowing Heather was on the verge of tears again. "It's none of my business."

Heather made a motion in the air with one hand. "No, no, it's okay. Talking about it helps."

Rebecca listened as Heather told of how Trevor moved her into his own home, a home he'd built himself in the country, and how he'd given Heather the job at the firm after his last secretary transferred to another state with her husband.

Her husband's parents were alive, having retired from the military and settled in Alaska to live out their golden years. Trevor was the oldest child at twenty-six. Her husband had been twenty-one.

"Trevor told me I could stay as long as I needed," she added.

Were they talking about the same Trevor Houston? Rebecca wondered. He shielded Heather like a mare shielded her colt. There was a basic goodness to him that appealed to her, a Christian spirit of caring. But when she caught his gaze thrown her way, it held no tenderness. He didn't trust her. She was living a lie and he knew it.

Rebecca stood and meandered to the refrigerator, pulled the freezer door open, and drew out a small container of chocolate ice cream. After retrieving a spoon from one of the kitchen drawers, she retreated to the bar and climbed atop a stool. Ice cream always made her feel better. A smile suddenly crossed her lips as a pleasant memory crossed her mind.

"Maria," she whispered into the air. She remembered all the times she and Maria had spent over bowls of chocolate ice cream, Rebecca's favorite. Warm milk and bubble baths were other mood boosters Maria had used.

A knock sounded on the door, startling Rebecca from her daydreams. She hesitated. Who could that possibly be? She didn't know anybody in the city well enough to be having visitors. The knock sounded again, stronger this time. Rebecca scooted the ice cream container toward the center of the bar and with spoon still in hand, padded softly, cautiously to the front door.

On the tips of her toes, she peered with one curious green eye through the door's eye hole. Her heart lurched in her chest. Trevor! The scowl on his face told her he wasn't here to pay a friendly visit.

Her gaze withdrew to the brass door knob as yet a third knock sounded. *Should I just pretend I'm not home? No, he's surely seen my car parked in the carport out front.*

Realizing she had no choice but to let him in, she scanned her appearance. Ugh! Her hair was pulled back in a high pony tail. She wore an oversized T-shirt over jeans, slouchy socks, and not a stitch of makeup.

Inhaling deeply, Rebecca grasped the knob and give it a swift turn, yanking the door open before she could reconsider.

"Hi!" She tried to sound cheery but saw it had absolutely no effect on his hard features. He marched in without being invited and immediately scanned the surroundings.

Rebecca closed the door and pulled her bottom lip in between her teeth. No sense pretending everything was well and fine. The obvious was right in front of her eyes.

"I know it isn't much," she told him. "Just bought the furniture today." She absentmindedly twirled the spoon nervously with her fingers.

Trevor examined the kitchen, but disapproval washed over his face when he averted his gaze to the melting ice cream that had begun to spill its contents onto the bar. Rebecca saw it too and after grabbing a dish cloth began to clean up the puddle of gooey chocolate mingling with melted frost.

"Who are you?"

Rebecca suddenly wished her father were here to protect her, as he had when Candace wanted to scold her for reasons he felt inadequate. But he wasn't. She drew in a deep breath and extended an open palm toward the new sofa.

"Would you care for a seat?"

"Just answer the question."

"It's a long story. If you'll just have a—"

"Answer the question!"

Rebecca had never heard him yell before. Nor had she ever seen him angrier.

"I'm trying," she retorted, "but I can't explain anything to you when you're like this!" Her words equaled his in animation and pitch as a flood of warmth washed through her body.

"At least what you see is what you get." His tone was accusing. He dug a thick, well manicured hand through his dark curls. One springy ebony lock dangled just above his right eye.

Rebecca crossed in front of him and plopped down onto the sofa. If he wasn't going to sit, she surely was. If she stood much longer she might faint, and she certainly didn't want him to know how vulnerable she was.

Still twirling the spoon, she said, "Why don't you tell me what you know? I'll try to fill in the details."

Rebecca had known in her heart that this day would come, but she could never have known how difficult it would be. She would probably lose her job. Yet, deep inside, she was glad to get it over. She would not have to live a lie any longer.

"And I suppose you expect me to believe you when you fill in the details," he enunciated.

Feeling her anger mount, Rebecca drew in a sharp breath and narrowed her eyes. How dare he? He had no idea of what her past held and why her future was permeated with half-truths. It was never her desire to go this route. She would never have chosen it on her own. No! Her uncle had done the choosing for her!

But Trevor spoke before she could respond.

"Wesbrook. . .Rebecca Wesbrook, only child. . .adopted, father an important businessman, seeking a divorce."

Rebecca's eyes widened as she interrupted his string of details concerning her life. "Divorce?"

"Yes!" Trevor nearly shouted. "And your mother's name is Candace. She and your father's twin brother have plans to exchange nuptials as soon as the divorce is final."

Feeling herself go limp, Rebecca was glad she was sitting down. "Divorce," she repeated under her breath as though Trevor were not in the room. "Marrying my uncle?" Saliva thickened in her throat making it difficult to swallow.

Trevor grew passive, but only for a moment, as though studying her reaction. "No, ma'am," he argued. "You can't pull one over on me now."

Rebecca moistened her lips with her tongue and fought against the tears that edged her bottom lids. When she finally did speak, her voice quaked.

"I'm not trying to." She struggled with her words. "How did you find all this out?"

"I'm a lawyer, remember? I'm paid to investigate. But I also had a little help," he continued, making a visible effort to curb his anger. "I have a friend, a private investigator friend. When I checked into your social security number and discovered you weren't who you said you were, I had him check you out—at great length." He flashed perfect white teeth. "I know everything about you, Ms. Wesbrook."

Her heart quickened. Did he know? But he continued before she could ponder further.

"You play a mean game of tennis. You ranked in the top of your class in school and you're forfeiting a once-in-a-lifetime college scholarship. Yale?"

"All of it's true." Something about getting it all out, everything about her life—good, bad, and painful—felt right. The feeling stemmed from the core of truth taught her as a child. No mere man could take away the foundation her Christian upbringing had given her, but the rape had shaken the walls more than she cared to admit. She'd let him fire her and attempt to sort her world out from there. Right now, shame and shock overrode her capacity to argue. Yet, his next words told her he knew nothing about the rape, providing some relief.

"I think you're running away from all of that. I think you can't handle the divorce, and runaway emotions led you here." Trevor paused, as though thinking, and rubbed his hairline. His thick, dark brows drew together, making creases in his forehead.

Divorce? He thought she had run away because Shane and Candace were in a messy divorce. She nearly laughed.

Rebecca listened as Trevor told her about Maria, Briann, and Jimmy, and even minor acquaintances. He knew things like who she had gone to the prom with, and how late she stayed out at night, but to Rebecca's relief, he never mentioned much about her uncle except that he was an alcoholic.

As the minutes dragged on, Rebecca noticed some of the fire leaving Trevor's words. She felt bad for having lied in the first place and knew he had every right to be angry, even fire her. But he never did. She sensed the interview was nearing an end when he moved toward the entry door. But he had one more thing to get off his mind before he left.

"Things in life are not always easy to deal with," his tone softened, "but, we can't run away from our problems. God allows these things to happen so we can learn from them. And your mother doesn't need this pain, especially with her pregnancy. I hope you get in contact with your family soon and get all this sorted out." With that he was gone.

eleven

Giving the key a fitful turn, Rebecca unlocked the suite door. She thought it odd that Heather wasn't yet in the office. Her friend always beat her there in the mornings and usually had coffee and tea ready for them both when Rebecca arrived promptly at eight. Just as she tugged the door open, she heard Heather's melodious voice behind her.

"Hold the door!" she bellowed playfully. "I'm coming!"

Just as Heather waddled into the office, Rebecca's knees went weak. *Does Heather know? Has Trevor told her?* Rebecca wanted to be the one to tell her friend, but she worried about how that knowledge might affect their friendship. Heather would have every right to distrust her. But Heather showed no signs of knowing and Rebecca relaxed.

"I guess you're wondering why I'm late this morning," Heather joked. She dropped her purse beside the desk and plopped into her desk chair.

"Is everything okay?" Rebecca asked out of concern for Heather's unusual tardiness.

Heather ran her hand in circular motions over the blue denim jumper covering her bulging tummy. "Braxton Hicks," she said matter-of-factly.

"Who is that?"

"Not who, what. Contractions."

Rebecca leaned across the desk, drawing her face closer to Heather's. "You're in labor?"

Chuckling, Heather shook her head.

Rebecca dropped into the seat opposite the desk, relief showing on her face.

"I'm having false contractions," Heather explained. "It's common for most women, and the doctor says it's nothing to be concerned about."

Rebecca forgot about her own problems. "Did the doctor examine you?"

"Trevor took me in last night." As though sensing Rebecca's distress she added, "Everything's okay. The doctor may move my Cesarean date up a smidge, but that's all."

Rebecca took a deep breath and stood. "Thank God, you're all right!" She fingered the string of pearls that hung at the base of her throat, matching the beige cotton dress she wore. "Can I get you some tea?"

"Is there any apple spice left?" Heather asked as she turned the computer on and began shuffling papers.

"One bag. I checked yesterday."

She meandered through Trevor's office and into the small adjoining room equipped with sink, bathroom, counter, and Coke machine. Her hands began to shake as she poured grounds into the automatic coffee maker and started a second pot of water on a second burner for Heather's herbal tea.

What if Trevor walks in while I'm back here? How can I face him now that he knows? Somehow, she reasoned, *I would have been better off had he just fired me.*

As though hearing her thoughts, Heather yelled through the office, "Trevor won't be in today!"

Rebecca carried the steaming beverages into the front office and placed them gently on the desk. Heather took hers and sipped from it gingerly. "Where is he?" Rebecca asked softly, not wanting to appear stressed.

"Austin," Heather answered. "He had an emergency meeting with the Gladstone Trading Company. Something about a hostile takeover. He'll be back on Wednesday."

"Oh," was all Rebecca offered. She didn't want Heather to sense how relieved she was.

"I'll need you to call all of our clients scheduled for appointments today and cancel. He has also scheduled to have lunch with a friend. Cancel that, too."

Rebecca's heart quickened. Could that be the private investigator he'd mentioned Saturday? She dragged the oversized chair to the other side of the desk and positioned herself opposite the phone. After unlocking the bottom drawer, she drew the large brown appointment book from its base and began thumbing through pages until she found the day's date.

Keeping an index finger on the first entry, she lifted the phone's receiver. That was as far as she got.

Heather doubled over in her chair and then dropped to her hands and knees on the carpeted office floor. As Rebecca dropped the receiver and knelt at Heather's side, she heard a strange swishing sound. The light brown carpet beneath Heather darkened as it became saturated with fluid.

Panic consumed Rebecca. "What's going on? What's wrong?"

All Heather could do was groan. Then she sucked in a shallow breath and turned an agonized face toward Rebecca. "The baby," she wheezed. "The baby's coming."

"Coming? No!"

Grasping her abdomen, Heather's face contorted in agony as yet another pain surged through her body. "Ambulance," she choked.

Rising from her knees, Rebecca grabbed the phone's receiver and dialed 911. She shouted the address into the mouth-piece and was asked to hold the line. The cord didn't reach far and Rebecca was forced to go back and forth between the emergency operator and Heather.

"The baby's coming!" Heather screeched as she rolled onto her side. More fluid escaped.

Rebecca knew then what she must do. She dropped the phone, grabbed her purse and car keys, and helped Heather to her feet. "I'm taking you to the hospital before it's too late!"

Rebecca knew the situation was critical. Heather suffered from toxemia which could be fatal if untreated, fatal for Heather and the baby. She helped Heather into the back seat of her car and floored the gas pedal.

Heather cried weakly, "Help me!"

Within ten minutes, Rebecca arrived at the emergency entrance of Northwest Texas Hospital. She threw open the car door and dashed through the automatic doors yelling for help. A nurse dressed in traditional hospital white rushed out from behind a cloth screen and ran toward Rebecca who motioned toward the Porsche.

"My friend's baby is coming!" she gasped. The nurse and two attendants followed Rebecca to the car.

"Name?" the nurse asked calmly. Heather was placed securely in a wheel chair and wheeled through the emergency room doors.

"Name?" Rebecca whispered, confused. "Oh. Heather, Heather Houston," she finally managed.

"Doctor?"

"I don't know," Rebecca choked as she watched her friend disappear down a hall and through a set of double doors.

"You might want to use the waiting room on the maternity ward," a kind voice hinted after she collapsed into a chair by the emergency room entrance.

Rebecca straightened her posture and dabbed at a runaway tear. She found herself looking into the soft brown eyes of a woman in her mid-sixties, impeccably groomed and dressed in a dusty rose jacket over white polyester slacks. A pin on her lapel identified her as Mattie, one of the many hospital volunteers.

"Maternity ward?" Rebecca asked.

"Isn't she about to have a baby?"

Rebecca suddenly felt foolish. "Oh. Yes. Can you tell me where the maternity ward is?"

The woman smiled serenely. "I can do more than that." She patted Rebecca gently on the shoulder and motioned her to follow.

The heavy scent of antiseptic flooded her nostrils as she was led through a maze of halls with highly polished floors. Stretchers with thin pads covered by blue blankets were placed strategically along walls. Nurses and attendants wove their way through the maze with IV bottles, pill cups, and extra pillows and blankets.

After boarding an elevator that piloted them to the third floor, Rebecca entered a cozy room lined with chairs. A television was high on a shelf in the corner of the room, with the volume turned completely down. About seven people, four at one end of the room, three at the other, hovered close to each other and talked in controlled tones, oblivious to Rebecca's arrival.

After Rebecca seated herself, the woman asked for the name of their doctor.

"I'm not sure." Rebecca drew her shoulders up for effect.

"What's your sister's name?"

Rebecca smiled. "She's not my sister; she's a good friend. Her name is Heather Houston."

"That should do it," said Mattie. "I'll let them know you're here. The doctor will contact you as soon as things take shape."

Rebecca stood and offered her hand. "Thank you so much, Mattie. I don't know what I would have done without you."

"No, no," Mattie argued. "That's what I'm here for." She stepped across the threshold and back into the bright fluorescent lights that made her meticulously groomed gray hair appear purple. "Now, if you need coffee or soft drinks while you wait, just follow the signs. There are also sandwich and snack machines in the concession room. Or you can go to the cafeteria for a hot lunch."

"What about a phone?"

"Straight down this hall." She pointed and Rebecca caught sight of a pay phone. With that, Mattie was gone.

Taking a much-needed breath, Rebecca relaxed her

tense muscles in an effort to calm herself. She looked at her watch. Only ten minutes had passed since her arrival at the hospital, but it seemed an eternity. She pondered her next step and shuddered visibly. She must reach Trevor.

Rebecca rummaged through her purse and was able to scrape together a dollar's worth of change. She stood, smoothed her dress, and made her way down the hall, her low heels clacking loudly on the hard tile floor. When she reached the phone, she lifted the receiver, inserted a quarter, and punched Austin information to get Gladstone Trading's number.

The woman's voice that answered for the Austin corporation sounded far off.

"I need to reach Mr. Trevor Houston," Rebecca said in a tone now steady with confidence. She realized that she had to think of Heather at this time and not herself.

The phone crackled in the background as the voice came back on. "I'm sorry. Mr. Houston will be in meetings all day. May I take a message?"

"This is an emergency," she declared. "I need to speak with him immediately."

The voice sounded even more distant. "May I ask what the emergency is?"

"His sister-in-law's at the hospital. She's had some complications with her pregnancy. Notify him immediately!"

Suddenly the voice seemed stronger, as though the woman's interest had been piqued in some way.

"May I have your name and a number you can be reached at?"

"Rebecca Wood." She hesitated. "I'm sorry. Wesbrook, Rebecca Wesbrook." She suddenly realized the lie had become all too real. "I'm at Northwest Texas Hospital on the maternity ward. Have him call me as soon as possible."

Having hung the phone up, she turned toward the hall and followed the signs to the concession room. Coins clanked against metal as Rebecca dropped them in the appropriate slot and punched the jutting lip of the Coke machine. She popped the top and took an extended sip from the syrupy liquid, allowing it to moisten her parched throat.

Only minutes after she sat back down in the waiting room, Mattie's face appeared at the waiting room entrance. Her deep brown gaze caught Rebecca's attention.

"You have a phone call at the desk."

Breezing past her, Rebecca bridged the gap to the nurses' station with coltish strides. A nurse handed her the receiver and punched a lit button.

"This is Rebecca," she offered warily, knowing full well the caller's identity. Trevor's tone was wrought with concern.

"Rebecca? How's Heather? Is she—"

"I'm not sure yet, Trevor. I wish I could answer that."

"Has the doctor been to see you yet?"

Rebecca frowned as she heard him suck in a distressed breath.

"I don't know anything yet," she offered, her voice soft. She wished she could offer him some glimmer of hope, but she couldn't. Rebecca explained in detail what had transpired until the point when Heather had been taken away in a wheelchair. A brief pause ensued as though Trevor were deep in thought. When he spoke, it was with intention.

"I'll be on the next flight out of Austin. Stay there with her until I arrive. Please!"

"Of course," Rebecca said. "I'll be here." The line went dead.

After returning to her seat in the waiting room, Rebecca lowered her head and prayed for her friend. Then, against her will, her thoughts drifted back to Saturday. So much had happened to the people she left behind in such a brief time and she ached for them.

She also thought about the baby Candace now carried. Trevor was wrong about her feelings toward the unborn child. Her problem was with Candace and Kane. A tear rolled down her flushed cheek as she thought about the baby being in the care of two human beings who had no right to have a child. More hot tears flashed from her steady gaze as she considered how hurt Shane must be from all this, and realized she hadn't helped matters any by running away.

Fresh tears sought freedom from her long lashes, only to splash and disintegrate on her dress. Then she heard the noise.

Mattie and a man dressed in green scrubs were hustling down the hall straight for her. Rebecca guessed him to be the physician.

The soda can crackled beneath her grip as she met the doctor's gaze—intense and filled with concern.

"Are there any family members with whom I can talk?"

he asked.

Rebecca stood and left her soda on the small table by her chair. She approached Mattie and the doctor who led her out into the corridor. "No. Not yet. But I'm a good friend."

"She brought her here," Mattie interjected helpfully.

The doctor paused for a brief moment as though choosing his words carefully. When he finally spoke, the blood in Rebecca's veins ran cold.

"We have a problem."

twelve

"A girl!" Rebecca gasped as the doctor gave her the news. Her excitement dimmed when she saw the concern in his eyes, gazing at her over a pair of black bifocals. Beads of sweat projected like tiny blisters at his receding hairline and above his upper lip.

"We're not out of the woods yet," he informed her.

Rebecca raked her hand through her tangled locks. "What is it? Heather? The baby?"

"The baby's doing just fine," the doctor continued. "Her birth weight is lower than I'd like, but she's adjusting to life outside the womb just fine for now."

Rebecca drew a shallow breath. "Heather?"

The doctor removed his bifocals. "Mrs. Houston has a condition known as toxemia. Actually," he continued, "in late pregnancy, it's call preeclampsia. This is what has caused her puffiness, her swollen fingers, legs, even eyelids."

Rebecca nodded understanding.

"Mrs. Houston's blood pressure is extremely high right now. During the delivery she lost consciousness and began convulsing. We weren't able to remove the baby surgically, as planned. She was fully dilated and the baby's head had already crowned." He paused. "She's conscious now, but she's not responding to the medication we've given her."

"And if she doesn't respond?" Rebecca asked, worry lines creasing her forehead.

"If she doesn't respond soon, we've got real problems."

"What kind of problems?"

Suddenly, the doctor changed the subject. "Removing the baby from the body should have brought Heather around. Some women's bodies fail to adjust to the metabolic and physiological stresses of pregnancy. The delivery of the child generally resolves this problem. It could very well be that Mrs. Houston is coming out of it more slowly. We may simply have a wait on our hands."

Leaning back against the wall, Rebecca asked, "What now?"

"Well, I'd like to get hold of a family member."

"Her brother-in-law's in Austin, but he's taking the next flight out. I'm sure he'll get in touch with Heather's family and his own parents."

The doctor gripped the bridge of his nose between his thumb and forefinger. "Will you leave word at the nurses' station the minute he arrives?"

"Absolutely."

After replacing his bifocals, the doctor extended his right hand. The hand was warm to the touch and Rebecca drew strength through its firm grip.

"I'll keep you informed as things develop." He turned to leave.

"Wait!"

He paused, glancing back over his shoulder at her.

"When can I see her?"

"I'll let you know. We have to get her stabilized first." Then he was gone on energetic legs while Rebecca stood alone, every part of her body permeated with exhaustion.

The hot lunch of steak and fried potatoes restored some of Rebecca's energy. When the elevator doors opened she ambled to the front desk to check on her friend's condition.

Her eyes glanced quickly to the clock on the wall inside the nurses' cubicle. One o'clock. Just as she was ready to inquire about Heather, she caught sight of a familiar figure stepping off the elevator.

Her heart sank when he approached the nurses' station without noticing her. He dropped his luggage on the floor with a thud and leaned slightly over the upper lip of the desk that surrounded the cubicle.

"Where's my sister-in-law? Heather Houston? Can I see her?"

The nurse spoke calmly. "And you are?"

"Her brother-in-law. Trevor Houston."

She laid the chart on the desk in front of her. "I'm sure everything's just fine, Mr. Houston. I'll see if I can round up Heather's doctor for you."

As the nurse turned her attention to the intercom, Rebecca was able to scan Trevor's disheveled appearance—from his loosened tie and wrinkled suit pants, to a shadow of a beard that clung to his strong jaw line.

"Trevor?" The surprised look on his face when he faced her caught Rebecca off guard.

"Rebecca?" he asked as though he hadn't seen her in years. "I'm sorry," he offered, obviously sensing her chagrin, "Thank God, you're still here."

Rebecca swallowed hard to keep her emotions in check.

"Where else would I be?" *Doesn't he know how much I care for Heather? Haven't enough days gone by to show I'm not some irresponsible brat only concerned about myself?*

He paused for a moment. "I'm sorry," he said, grazing the stubble on his chin with his thumb and forefinger.

Rebecca accepted his apology and bent to grasp the smaller of the leather bags. "Here, let me help you."

Gathering the two heavier bags in strong hands, Trevor allowed Rebecca to lead him into the empty waiting room. Taking her usual seat, she motioned for Trevor to take one also.

A stark silence loomed over them.

Finally Trevor broke in. "Have you heard anything yet?"

His eyes mirrored his anguish when he posed the question and Rebecca wanted to take his hand in hers, somehow take his pain and make it her own. She knew that would be impossible. All she could offer was support and her faith, which she had only recently discovered was her only source of comfort in times such as these. "I've been waiting to hear since I last spoke with the doctor." She shrugged her shoulders. "There's been no word. But I've prayed for her, Trevor. It's in God's hands."

When he dropped his head into his palms and rubbed his eyes, Rebecca touched his shoulder. Suddenly she felt uncomfortable. "Maybe the doctor will know something soon," she offered, retrieving her hand and caging it with the other in her lap.

Surprisingly, the doctor appeared in the doorway,

exhaustion beginning to leave bags beneath his beady eyes. "Mr. Houston?" he asked, looking at Trevor.

Trevor rose from his chair, standing a full head above the doctor. Bending slightly forward at the waist, he offered one large hand which the doctor took. "Dr. Bomgard. It's good to see you again."

Trevor had accompanied Heather on several of her office visits and knew the doctor by appearance only. The words Dr. Bomgard spoke next brought a look of instant relief to Trevor's tortured features.

"Heather's out of danger."

Rebecca rose to her feet as though standing would somehow help the good news to sink in better.

"Her blood pressure has dropped and seems to be stabilized. If she does well for the next couple of hours, we'll move her out of ICU and into a private room on the maternity ward. You're welcome to visit with her for ten minutes, Mr. Houston." He turned to Rebecca. "I'm sorry. Only family is allowed in intensive care." Then he was gone.

The breath Trevor released was full and long as though it held all the frustration and fear he'd endured for the past several hours. He turned to face Rebecca. "You're welcome to go home if you'd like."

The kindness in his tone filled her with new insight. She cared what this man thought and felt about her. Rebecca nodded and pulled her hair back off her shoulders. "I could stay if you'd like," she offered, willing to do whatever he needed. She liked him, plain and simple.

Spearing fingers through his unruly tangle of ebony curls, Trevor searched her eyes. "You've done enough.

Besides, you look tired and in need of rest. Go home."

Her black clutch was on the chair behind her and when Rebecca reached for it, she felt a strong hand grip her arm and spin her gently around. At first she was startled, but when she saw his eyes held no maliciousness, she relaxed.

"I just wanted to say thanks," said Trevor, releasing his grip and dropping his hand into his pocket, jingling keys as he did.

Rebecca smiled and touched his shoulder, confidently this time. "There's no need," she said. "I love Heather."

She retrieved her purse and moved toward the door. "Please tell her I'm praying for her. And call me when she gets out of intensive care. I want to see her and the baby."

The look of surprise that suddenly engulfed Trevor's features baffled Rebecca until she realized that Trevor knew nothing about the child. He had been on an airplane when the news was delivered.

"Baby?" Trevor asked.

A grin played on Rebecca's face as she backed toward the elevator. "I'll let Heather give you that news."

As the elevator doors closed between them, Rebecca vowed she would remember Trevor's expression for the rest of her life. It held a mixture of pain, relief, and total confusion. And his roughed up appearance only enhanced that impression. For once, she realized, Trevor Houston could feel something other than anger. He actually had a heart. This man knew how to love and love deeply, something that had suddenly become of paramount importance to Rebecca.

Traffic was slow and it took Rebecca nearly thirty minutes to reach the bank. She made several apologetic calls to clients. After locking up, she wove her way through the traffic to her apartment where she threw her tired body onto the bed and fell into the sweetest, deepest, dreamless sleep she had ever known.

thirteen

The shrill ring of the phone startled Rebecca awake. She stumbled down the hall in a stupor to where it hung on the wall separating the kitchen from the living area.

"Hello?" she asked, her voice a hoarse whisper.

Trevor sounded strong on the other end, the kindness she had sensed earlier still in his tone.

"They're moving her to a private room," he said. There was a pause. "Did I wake you?"

Laughing, Rebecca lightly scolded him. "I was sound asleep when you called. You should be ashamed."

His chuckle on the other end set her at ease. Something had changed between them, and she liked the new feelings blossoming inside her.

"You probably needed it. You looked beat."

"I *was* beat. I don't even remember falling asleep." Rebecca fluffed her tangled hair with her free hand and sighed. "Do I have enough time to grab a quick shower? I'm a mess."

"Sure. They won't be moving her for another thirty minutes or so. They're filling out the paper work right now. Just wanted to let you know."

Unlatching the pearls from around her throat, she asked, "How's Heather?"

"When I saw her, she looked awful; dark circles under her eyes, weak, pale. But the doctor says she's doing great—she and the baby both."

Rebecca basked in his words. "That's wonderful news! I'll be there in about an hour."

"Great! Heather has a surprise for you when you get here."

Rebecca's nose wrinkled as her brows shot downward. "A surprise for me? What is it?" The masculine laugh on the other end made her smile.

"Now if I told you, it wouldn't be a surprise, would it? When you get here, you'll see."

"I'm on my way." Rebecca padded to the bathroom. A shower was just what she needed to revive her.

It was already 4:00 P.M. when she stepped in the elevator. Rebecca stepped off on the third floor and her white sneakers squeaked against the meticulously clean tile floor as she strode to the nurses' station straight ahead of her.

New faces peered up at her and Rebecca realized the nursing staff had rotated. "I need Mrs. Houston's new room number." Rebecca couldn't remember feeling so content. Her friend made it through a life or death struggle and a new life had been added to her small circle of friends. And Trevor. . .

The nurse seized a white piece of paper from the top of a stack of pink, yellow, and white forms and scanned it with studious eyes. "She's in room 314."

Rebecca noted where the nurse pointed, offered a courteous nod for her help, and then bounded down the hall.

Heather's door was closed and when Rebecca lifted her knuckles to strike it, she heard muffled voices inside, belonging to Trevor and Heather. They seemed to be in deep conversation about something. Her heart throbbed in her chest. She almost walked away. What if they were talking about her—her past?

She was startled when she heard a soft voice say, "Come in." She didn't remember knocking, although her fist was still positioned by the door as though she were about to. It took all her effort to march in, feigning confidence.

"Rebecca!" Heather pushed herself upright and twisted her sore body slightly to offer a hug. Rebecca fell into that hug with no hesitation and drew strength from the warm embrace they shared, each feeling as though they had just survived a direct hit on the front lines of a battlefield.

In that instant, she realized Heather knew nothing of her past, but knew also that she would have to reveal it to her soon. She felt it important that Heather learn the truth from her and not discover it through other means. If the friendship died because of it, Rebecca must accept that. After all, the lie was her own fault. Either way, Heather deserved to know.

A warm smile thrown her way by Trevor slowed Rebecca's racing pulse. His new attitude toward her hadn't changed. Her brows arched upward in confusion, though, when Trevor donned his jacket and retrieved his abandoned tie from the bottom of the bed where it had been tossed.

"Going?" was all she could manage.

"Just to the ranch to get a few of Heather's things." He held up a small notebook with the entire first page written on. He laughed. "A *few* of her things. Can you spell me for awhile? It'll give me a chance to unpack and maybe grab a shower myself."

"Sure!" Rebecca said. "Take all the time you need." Then he breezed through the doorway, leaving the door slightly ajar when he left. Rebecca made a motion to close it.

"That's okay," Heather intercepted before she could reach it.

Rebecca shut it anyway. She had to talk to Heather about things she didn't want the rest of the world to hear. When she caught Heather's quizzical glance, Rebecca merely smiled. "I know this may sound rude, but, before we talk about you, we need to talk about me."

Heather grew silent, although her puzzled expression remained.

Rebecca returned to her bedside and sat down in a chair that Trevor had earlier occupied. She shifted into a comfortable position, crossed her ankles, and proceeded to indulge Heather. But, there was one thing Rebecca didn't tell her friend: the secret she would hold within her forever.

When she finished, nearly forty minutes had elapsed. She bit her bottom lip as she studied Heather's face and waited for the response she felt was due her betrayal.

Rebecca didn't understand the tears that slid from her friend's tired blue eyes. And when Heather held out a small, delicate hand, Rebecca took it in a daze.

"I'm so sorry," Heather offered. "You must be frightened."

"I am. . .I was. But wait." Rebecca shook her head in disbelief. "I'm the one who should be sorry. Aren't you angry?"

Heather caressed Rebecca's reddened cheek with her free hand while still holding Rebecca's hand with the other. "No," she said, "I'm honored."

"Honored!" Rebecca proclaimed. "How can you say that?"

"It's easy. You thought enough of our friendship, Rebecca, to confide in me. The past doesn't matter. The future does."

Rebecca paused, allowing Heather's wise words to sink in.

"You mean, I'm forgiven? You don't care about what I've done, or why I did it? I never told you why I did what I did. Trevor drew his own conclusion, whether right or wrong, but you act as though it doesn't matter."

"Of course it matters," Heather quickly corrected. "I already know *what* you've done, but the *why* of it all will come when you're ready. Otherwise, we'll wait."

Rebecca gripped both of Heather's petite hands, most of the swelling from the toxemia having subsided. She swallowed with difficulty as she spoke her next words. "And if I never tell you why, what then? Will you be able to trust me?"

Heather nodded.

"Why? I mean how? How can you trust me if I choose never to tell you the rest?"

"That choice is yours and yours alone," Heather answered. "The fact that you thought enough of our friendship to come forth with what you did says to me you *can* be trusted."

Rebecca stood and paced the floor. Then she approached Heather again and squared her shoulders. "You *can* trust me."

Heather smiled. "Bad things may happen in our lives, but God will always turn them around to good."

"I've heard that before," Rebecca said, remembering how her nanny, Maria, always quoted this from the Bible when things got rough around the Wesbrook Estate. Then her lips curved downward in a frown. "Do you really think something good will come of all this?" she asked, waving her hands in the air as though touching her invisible problems.

"With all my heart," Heather replied. Then a knock sounded at the door.

"Come in!" Heather called out.

Trevor entered, looking fresh and carrying two long white boxes. He handed one to each of them.

Rebecca took hers and mouthed, "For me?" Her eyes wide with curiosity, she opened the box and moved the delicate paper away. Beautiful roses lay in dainty repose, swathed in an array of baby's breath.

"Hey!" Rebecca reproached, smiling. "She's the new mommy, not me."

"But you helped me become one," Heather returned, fingering the velvety petals of one of her own roses. Trevor wasted no time adding to the conversation.

"The doctor gave us some news you ought to know."

"News?"

"Oh, it's good news now, although it wasn't at the time," Heather interjected.

She threw her glance from one to the other as they each spoke in turn.

"He told us if you hadn't gotten Heather to the hospital when you did, she might not be with us now,"

Trevor continued.

Rebecca stared blankly at Heather as though trying to digest all that was being said.

Heather picked up the dialogue. "He even said, the fact that the baby came early probably saved my life as well. He said my blood pressure had already skyrocketed out of control by the time I got out of bed this morning, maybe sooner. The only thing that saved me was the fact that the baby came when she did. The time it would have taken to prepare me for surgery would have killed me. Somebody was watching over me."

Her grip tightening around the box, Rebecca suddenly realized her prayer had been answered. When the doctor told her about Heather's condition during the delivery, she had reasoned to herself that God hadn't listened to her, that maybe she simply wasted precious air with her words. It occurred to her that God knew exactly what He was doing all along.

"Have you seen the baby?"

"No. Not yet," Rebecca offered modestly, although feeling slightly like a hero. "I haven't had a chance."

"Why don't you go to her now," said Heather, her face aglow with anticipation.

Taking her by the elbow, Trevor led Rebecca through the door. "I'll go with you."

Rebecca allowed herself to be led down another corridor and to a wall with large windows.

She peeked inside at all the tiny newborns that lay in tiny bassinets, some crying, some sleeping. "Where is she?" Rebecca asked when she couldn't locate the infant.

Trevor pointed to the south wall. "Right over there, last baby in the first row." He nudged Rebecca to the other side of the glass where she could get a better view. "See the sign taped to the end of her crib?"

As Rebecca scanned the little pink sign, her mouth suddenly dropped open. Trevor chuckled lightly at her expression. The sign read "Rebecca Diane Houston."

As though in answer to her thoughts, Trevor explained, "Diane is my mother's name. Heather wanted to name the baby after you because you saved her life. This is the surprise."

Rebecca turned to face him as glistening drops traveled down her flushed cheeks. The sight of little Rebecca made her think of her own mother, her real one. This baby girl was so blessed. She had a loving mother who would nurture her as she grew, and she would always know who she was. Rebecca ached to know her real identity. Did she look like her mother? Or her father? What about grandparents? What about brothers and sisters? The questions made her shiver and she folded her arms across her chest. Trevor's next words warmed her.

"She's an angel," he whispered.

"Yes, she is," Rebecca agreed. Then she caught Trevor's reflection in the glass. He was staring at *her*. "It's about dinner time," she said softly.

Rebecca could smell food. An awkward looking trolley lined with trays of food moved noisily through the corridor. Her stomach growled. "I'm starving."

"Why don't you and I go down to the cafeteria and get a bite to eat?" It was more a statement than a question.

Rebecca surprised herself by agreeing without hesitation.

"Good," Trevor said, taking one more quick peek at his niece. "I'll go tell Heather. Meet me at the elevator."

"I'll go with you. It isn't everyday I'm given the honor of a namesake." But the nurse was in the room and neither were allowed in.

As Rebecca took her seat opposite Trevor, she tried to avoid looking directly into his eyes. She couldn't fathom the fact that she was having dinner with the man who had coerced her into her present job; the man whose car she had dented; the man who'd paid a private investigator to check her out. And she couldn't control the unfamiliar emotions that rolled inside her like a flash flood.

She had seen his other side. She saw him as a loving, caring person who could be trusted, and someone who would always be there when things weren't going so well. Like now.

Rebecca watched as he brought his fork to his mouth and took in the lasagna, chewing it slowly, leaving no traces of it. That was the way he handled himself in business: very mannerly, not easy to read as he left no traces of his inner emotions around for others to see. But she saw some of these emotions while his guard was down. And she liked what she saw. But did he? Did he like what he saw in her?

Squeezing the wedge of lemon over her iced tea, Rebecca tried to change her pattern of thought. After all, how could he like what he saw in her? What he had already seen had not been her at all. One thought nearly paralyzed her: what if Trevor discovered the real reason she left? Could he deal with her past then?

His next words brought new emotions bubbling to the

surface. "You're free to leave the firm if you want," he said while dabbing at his mouth with a paper napkin. He had already finished his meal.

Rebecca had barely touched hers. "What?"

"I'm releasing you from our agreement concerning the damage to my car."

"Is it paid for?"

"As far as I'm concerned it is."

Rebecca ran her tongue over the tops of her white teeth. She secretly berated herself for her feelings of dismay. Hadn't she wanted her freedom from the beginning? And now she didn't?

Trevor folded his hands on the table in front of him, and leaned slightly forward. "You saved my sister's life," he spoke. "You owe me nothing."

"B. . .but, with Heather gone, what will you do? I mean, I'm pleased to know that I can move on, but I don't want to leave you hanging." She hoped she didn't sound as desperate as she felt.

"We'll be just fine." Something indefinable edged his tone.

She dropped her stricken gaze. "All right."

"Shall we get back to the new mommy?"

The two walked in silence back to the elevator that carried them up to Heather's floor.

After hearing all about the baby's first feeding, Rebecca feigned exhaustion and begged her departure. Before she left, she reached into her clutch and drew out her key chain. She pulled a silver key off the chain and handed it to Trevor who had politely walked her to the door.

"Here," she said. "I won't be needing this anymore." Then she turned to Heather once more, forced a grin, and filed past Trevor, heading straight to the elevator that was blurred by a sudden onslaught of tears.

She had a lot to consider, not the least of which was finding a new job.

fourteen

"Rebecca!"

A large masculine hand wedged itself between the elevator doors. *What more could he possibly want?* As the doors reopened, she stepped out and found herself face to face with Trevor. Meekly, she answered, "Yes?"

He dropped something solid into the palm of her hand. The befuddled look on her face brought a quick response.

"Will you stay?"

"But you just told me—"

"I know what I just told you," Trevor interrupted. "I had to tell you that. I can't hold you here against your will. If you stay, it must be your decision."

Rebecca never thought she would hear those words. "Why are you asking me to stay?" she asked curiously.

Rubbing his freshly shaven jaw between his forefinger and thumb, Trevor asserted, "You're an asset to the firm, Rebecca, and I mean that. You do good work. And your kindness to Heather makes me believe there's still good in this world." He started to say more, but stopped.

Rebecca wondered what his next words would have been. "Of course, I'll stay. With Heather staying home with the baby, you'll be needing somebody." She smiled, feeling content for the first time in months.

Trevor flashed her a brilliant smile back. "Great! I'll call you from here in the morning. Most of my time will be spent here with Heather until she gets out of the hospital." He threw his gaze toward Heather's room, then back to Rebecca. "We'll have to work around clients until then."

As Rebecca slipped into the opening doors of the elevator, a smile stretched from ear to ear.

❧

Rebecca checked her watch. It was three-thirty and Trevor had a strategy meeting scheduled in thirty minutes. Maybe an hour had passed since he had left the office to pick up Heather at the hospital. She was finally being released. They had kept her and the baby under observation for five days before allowing them the luxury of going home. Trevor's parents had arrived safely from Alaska, and Heather's mother had flown in from Virginia.

At 4:30, Rebecca was due at Amarillo College to meet with a counselor and deliver forms she'd filled out for a federal grant. The day after Heather had delivered her baby, Rebecca had decided to go back to school.

Holding a daytime job, it would take about three years to get her pre-law basics and her Associate of Arts degree. She didn't know where she'd attend after completing her degree, but that decision could wait.

Rebecca busied herself updating and transferring funds on the ledger sheet of several clients' accounts and didn't think twice when the door to the suite opened, figuring it was Trevor. But when she didn't hear his usual, "I'm rushed, I'm rushed," she looked up from her work.

"Hello, Rebecca," the newcomer said.

Rebecca was speechless. Slowly, her ability to form words returned.

"Candace," she croaked, her voice barely above a

whisper. Suddenly, her entire body shook with anger. "What are you doing here? How did you find me?"

Candace held up a hand in defense. "Wait a minute. I'll answer all of your questions if you'll calm down."

"Calm down! You expect me to calm down?" Rebecca narrowed her icy gaze at Candace. "I never wanted to see you again! Now get out of here!"

Her words echoed off the small office walls, and she realized she'd have to control herself. She didn't want anybody in the suites lining the corridor to hear her words.

Quietly, Candace removed her light brown wrap and laid it across the other chair that was parked by the spare computer table. She dropped a bulky tapestry bag colored in a variety of earth tones beside the chair before sitting and folding her hands calmly in her lap.

Rebecca took a moment to scan Candace's appearance—from her cheaply applied makeup to the run in one stocking. The large flowers on the dress did nothing to hide the small ball of life that formed beneath them.

Rebecca's limbs quaked. Candace was a partner in the destruction of her old life. But Rebecca had worked hard to create a new life with people she dearly loved. Was Candace here to destroy that as well? Then she noticed Candace's eyes mist and the older woman dropped her gaze to her folded hands. It occurred to Rebecca that something was different about the woman she had called Mom for so many years.

For a long moment, Candace stared at her hands and swallowed hard. When she finally spoke, it was with great difficulty.

"I'm very sorry, Rebecca. I. . .I was so wrong." She peered up at Rebecca as tears stretched glistening paths down her gaunt features. "So very, very wrong."

"We're talking about my life, here," Rebecca retorted. "*My life!* I lost everything! I don't want you here, Candace." The words, the anger sounded foreign to Rebecca and she begged God's pardon. But the hurt had a life of its own. *Please, God, help me find myself again.*

"You have every right to be angry with me, darlin—"

Rebecca nearly wrenched the very word from Candace's mouth. "Darling! Don't call me that!"

There was a pause before Candace spoke again, as though trying to figure out how best to say what she had come to say.

"I probably have no right to ask you to forgive me." Candace searched Rebecca's eyes. She threaded a weak, trembling hand through her blond hair. "I was an awful mother, just awful."

Rebecca couldn't speak. She was completely undecided on how to take Candace's apology. Was she sincerely sorry? If so, what had caused such a drastic transformation? Candace would have been the last person on earth she would have thought could change. Yet Rebecca found herself listening intently.

"What I did to you—the way I treated you was dreadful." Black mascara smudged beneath Candace's lower lashes and traveled the same path as her tears. "I can't make up for that, Rebecca, but I want you to know how I feel."

Rebecca blew out a heavy breath as she stood and leaned on the desk with both palms. "Why the sudden change?"

Candace dropped her gaze to her lap as though analyzing the large gold, orange, and brown flowers on her dress. "Maria had a lot to do with it," she finally offered, keeping her gaze to her lap. "And this baby," she added as she caressed the roundness of her abdomen. Then she looked at Rebecca.

Rebecca dropped into her chair and clasped her hands in front of her on the cluttered desk. "That doesn't tell me a thing," she stated. She hated being so abrupt, but caution was her only defense.

"I know," Candace proffered. "Let me try to explain." She drew a deep breath. "You see, Maria never gave up on me. Why? I don't know. I made so many mistakes. And I ruined a wonderful marriage to a wonderful man." She paused and fresh tears edged her bottom lids, making her gray eyes appear glassy.

"And I lost you." A fresh supply of burning tears found their freedom. She cleared her throat. "I also let jealousy control me, Rebecca. It hurt me to see how Shane loved you and to see how you loved him. And, stupidly, I thought tennis might bring us together. When I played well in tennis as a kid, my father was always happy, always attentive. I thought tennis could somehow bring that back to me again, that happiness, that attention. I was wrong."

Rebecca bit at her bottom lip. She had so many questions she wanted to ask, but Candace wasn't finished.

"It all started when I couldn't have a baby of my own. That did something to me. Can't quite explain what. I just know I wanted a baby growing inside of me like this one."

Rebecca winced as Candace patted her stomach.

"When you came as a replacement for that, I just couldn't accept it. I guess I couldn't accept you."

"And now you can?" Though she wanted to forgive, wanted to understand, the rejection she'd suffered took its own voice. "Now that you're pregnant with a child of your own?"

"It's not that way," Candace countered. "It's like the baby inside me helped open my eyes. And Maria," Candace added with a slight grin. "She kept calling me her 'lost soul.' Except she'd say it in Spanish. But I knew what it meant. And when my world fell apart, she supported me and talked me through it all. She helped me understand so much about myself, so much about you and so much about God. Maria brought me face to face with reality and it hit me hard, Rebecca, so very hard."

A tingle traveled the length of Rebecca's spine. It was as though Maria had some secret understanding of the universe that nobody else had. Maria and Heather would get along very well.

"Maria stayed with me at the estate when Shane left." As though sensing Rebecca's question, she added quickly, "I don't know where Shane is. Somewhere overseas maybe. Anyhow, when he learned you ran off, he grew so despondent. He searched and searched for you. When he couldn't find you, he stopped working, he lost weight, everything." Candace paused. "Then when he found me and his brother together. . ."

Rebecca bristled at her words, feeling as though she had just been slapped.

"Please let me finish," Candace pleaded, obviously sensing Rebecca's anger. "I know it was wrong. But I can't turn back the hands of time." She waited a moment, then continued, "The affair started long before Shane caught us together. And when he caught us we weren't doing anything; but still, it was pretty obvious. You see, I found out I was two months pregnant two days after your graduation. After that discovery, I stopped drinking immediately. Funny thing is, without the alcohol in my system, I was able to see clearly. Alcohol had dulled my senses so that I couldn't see Kane for the man he really is. But, without it. . ."

Candace swallowed hard and drew a deep, replenishing breath. "He used me to get to Shane. He abused Maria verbally and I—" Suddenly, Candace stopped.

Rebecca leaned forward, intent on hearing her next words. She watched as Candace placed a frail hand against her trembling lips.

"And I allowed it all to happen. It's all my fault." Candace sobbed openly.

Before Rebecca knew it, she was beside Candace, holding her head in her hands and stroking unkempt strands of Candace's pale hair. "Shhh," she whispered. "It's gonna be all right—Mom."

Candace peered into Rebecca's face, took Rebecca's hands in her own, and pulled her down to her knees, meeting eye-to-eye.

"But it's not all right," she despaired. "Because I didn't believe you when you told me what he did to you." Her whole body shook with sobs.

Rebecca allowed her own tears to flow unbidden.

"You were crying out for help and I didn't listen," Candace whispered hoarsely. She covered her face with her hands.

Moments later, Candace's shoulders stopped quaking. She lifted her swollen eyes to Rebecca. "I'm so glad I found you." She smiled through her tears.

A question formed in Rebecca's mind. "How did you find me?"

"I was balancing the checkbook one day and came across the check Shane wrote out to you for graduation. *Amarillo* was stamped on the back along with the name of the business that cashed it. I knew how badly you wanted to attend college, how badly you wanted to become a lawyer. I came to Amarillo and checked out the colleges. One of them confirmed your application, and after giving them proper identification to prove I was your mother, they gave me the information I needed. That included your residence and your place of employment."

Rebecca's brows lifted, forming two perfect arches above her heavily lashed green eyes. She couldn't believe how easily she'd been found. "When did you get here?"

"Today. It took me a couple of hours to locate you."

"So, you don't have a place to stay?"

Candace shook her head, "No."

Rebecca made a suggestion she never thought she'd hear herself making. "You're welcome at my place, if you like."

Candace neither accepted nor declined the offer. "I have another question to pose before we discuss lodging." Candace continued hesitantly. "When I saw Kane for who he is, I couldn't marry him. I broke off our relationship. Unfortunately, he's fighting me for custody of the baby when it's born."

"I'm sorry," Rebecca offered, knowing how difficult that must be for Candace. She knew it wasn't the baby Kane wanted. No. He was after revenge. But nothing could prepare Rebecca for what Candace said next.

"I need your help," the older woman said. "I need you to testify on my behalf that Kane raped you, so that I can keep my baby."

Rebecca's hands grew clammy. Just then, Rebecca caught movement out of the corner of her eye. Somebody was standing just outside the office door that had been left slightly ajar. She adjusted her denim skirt and approached the door with determined steps. When she gripped the knob and pulled it open, all color drained from her face.

fifteen

Trevor brushed past her in silence and hurried to his office. Before closing the door, he angled his head toward Rebecca, who still held the doorknob tightly in her grip, and shot her a look she couldn't define. Rebecca's knees buckled and she nearly collapsed to the floor.

"Coffee pot's full," was all she could say.

"Thanks," Trevor offered before adding, "You're welcome to go home now. I can handle the meeting on my own."

Did he feel sorry for her? The last thing she wanted was somebody's pity. So he knew. What could she do about it now? If it changed their relationship, so be it.

As Rebecca dialed the number for the college to cancel her appointment, she nearly forgot about Candace, who sat motionless and withdrawn—so unlike the Candace she had once known.

Completing the task, Rebecca inserted a disk into the computer and ran through a series of steps to complete the backup sequence. The soft hum of the computer gave way to silence. Still Candace didn't move.

"Let's go," Rebecca said abruptly, grabbing her clutch.

Candace grasped her tapestry bag, her purse, and her wrap and followed like an obedient child.

Gray clouds swirled menacingly overhead as the women left the shelter of the bank. Before they could reach Rebecca's Porsche, a heavy downpour broke loose.

They dashed to the car. As Rebecca opened the passenger door with her key, she was stunned at Candace's reaction to the rain. Instead of using the huge tapestry bag as a shield against the pelting drops, she shielded it under her right arm.

What's in that bag? Rebecca fired the engine, refusing to dwell on the mystery. Other, more important things, needed her attention.

"Your car will be fine here tonight," she told Candace as she sped away.

The drive home was tense, not only from the blinding rain, but from lack of conversation. Not a word passed between the two women. When they stood dripping and cold by the door of Rebecca's apartment, Rebecca found her voice again. "I'll get a towel."

By the time Rebecca returned with a big, warm towel, Candace was shivering uncontrollably. Her belongings had been placed neatly on the section of tile in front of the door.

Rebecca narrowed her gaze at Candace. "You okay?"

"Guess I've lost so much weight, I don't have any insulation left," she half-joked.

Rebecca forced a chuckle. "How 'bout a hot shower?"

"Are you sure you want me here?"

Biting at her bottom lip, Rebecca paused, thinking. Did she want Candace here? Did it make a difference that she had apologized? Yet, how could she throw the woman out into the rain? And what about the baby? No! She had once needed a stranger's care. So did Candace's baby.

"You don't have much choice," she mustered, taking the damp towel Candace handed back to her.

"Then we need to talk."

"We can do that later. Right now, we need to get you warm."

Candace didn't argue as she followed Rebecca toward the bathroom.

"Use whatever you need. I'll get you an extra nightgown, robe, and a pair of socks." Then it occurred to her. "Have you eaten?"

"No, but that's—"

Rebecca interrupted her. "I'll have some chicken soup ready when you finish." With that, she got out the needed clothing and toiletries, handed them to Candace, and wove her way to the kitchen.

She set the heat on medium under the small sauce pan and moved closer to the blue and orange flame. Tiny bumps prickled the skin on her arms as the fire warmed her. When she turned toward the refrigerator to retrieve a previously opened sack of crackers and some sliced cheese, something caught her eye.

The objects Candace set by the door had been tampered with. Only the wrap and the purse were still there. Candace had taken the tapestry bag with her.

Just as Rebecca poured steaming chicken bits, noodles, and broth into two brown, stoneware bowls, Candace emerged from the bathroom. The hot steam from the shower had rosied her cheeks and her eyes looked clearer, more alert. The nightgown and robe fit her perfectly, as did the socks. Rebecca hadn't realized how close in size they were to each other. "Feel better?"

"Much. Thank you."

The meal was eaten in silence until the spoons clinked against empty bowls. Rebecca wasn't surprised when

Candace spoke first, echoing an earlier plea.

"Can we talk now?" she asked.

Rebecca busied herself with gathering the used dishes. "What is there to talk about?" she asked, running the water.

"Please!"

Stopping the stream of tepid water, Rebecca turned to face the woman. The agony she heard in that one word was something she couldn't ignore. Nor could she ignore the anger that fought to possess her.

Taking her seat, she noticed the tapestry bag rested on the table, nearly blocking her view of Candace.

"What's with the bag?" she quizzed, growing annoyed by its ominous presence. It obviously had something to do with her and she was tired of wasting time, even anticipated Candace's departure. *Forgive,* Rebecca silently reminded herself.

"That will come later," Candace offered as she rested one thin, pale hand atop the tote.

"Fine," Rebecca answered smartly. "What comes first?"

"I need an answer to the question I asked you earlier at the office." Candace cleared her throat. "Will you testify?"

"No."

"What?"

"I said, no." Rebecca didn't falter, even when Candace's gray eyes glazed with tears.

"Why won't you help me?" Candace's voice quaked.

"Why should I?"

"I said I was sorry, Rebecca. Can't you accept that?"

Rebecca ran a glossy nail over the tiny dip that formed

her upper lip. She remembered how Heather had forgiven her. After all, which was the worse sin? Neglect or deceit? And forgiveness, if given, must be complete. Not half-hearted. "Yes, I can accept that. And I forgive you."

Candace released a suppressed breath that Rebecca felt was premature. "Then you'll help me?"

"I said that I forgave you. But I won't testify for you."

"What about the baby? If not for me, for the baby."

"I'm sorry about your situation," Rebecca asserted. "But I want nothing to do with it. I've put my past behind me, and my testifying in court would only bring it to the surface again." She fingered a damp curl. "Besides, I don't want that part of my life laid open for the world to see. You must understand that."

"I do," stressed Candace, "but if it means—"

"If it means what?" Rebecca interjected.

"If it means that your sister or brother would be safe from that, that man."

"Wait a minute," charged Rebecca. "Don't use guilt on me. Besides, that isn't my sister or brother. I was adopted. Remember?"

"You're still my child!" Candace insisted.

"Well, why didn't you claim me when you had me?" Rebecca raked a hand through her damp hair. "You didn't even want me." Silvery tears flooded her lower lids.

"But I do now," whispered Candace, choking on tears that already wet paths down her face.

"Because you're desperate."

"That's not true!"

"So what's changed?"

"Me."

"You don't know what you're asking."

"I know that I'm asking a lot of you, Rebecca, but not for me, not just for me. I'm asking for the sake of this baby, this innocent life."

Chewing on her bottom lip, Rebecca dropped her gaze to the floor. Deep inside, she knew Candace was right. She couldn't allow Kane the remotest possibility of gaining custody over this child. But stopping him meant telling her story to a judge! Just as she was about to speak, Candace popped the snap open on the tapestry bag. Rebecca fell silent, her attention focused on the bag.

Candace searched Rebecca's eyes. "Look, don't give me your answer now. Think on it. Sleep on it. But, one way or another, I'll need your answer tomorrow. The deposition is two weeks from now. My lawyer wants to meet with each witness individually before the hearing which has been tentatively scheduled for next month. I'll need to get back to Houston to prepare for it."

Rebecca nodded as Candace continued.

"And I want you to know that, either way, I still want you to have these things."

Rebecca's forehead creased in confusion as she watched Candace pull out what looked to be a very old quilt, a single photograph, some yellowed sheets of paper, and an antique brass pocket watch.

"Whose are those?" she asked.

"They're yours," Candace answered. "Relics from your past, from your other family."

Rebecca made slow, stiff strides to her chair opposite Candace and sat, staring at the objects in front of her, afraid to touch them. Things were moving too fast for her to keep up, yet time seemed to stand still.

Finally, the luster of the pocket watch teased her into touching it. She gripped it between trembling fingers, letting its long gold chain dangle.

"That's from your father." Candace broke through the spell of the moment as Rebecca wove the watch's chain through her fingers. "There are initials engraved on the inside."

Opening it, Rebecca stared at the initials, unable to comprehend their meaning.

"Your father's initials," Candace said in answer to Rebecca's silent question.

Rebecca poured her gaze over the letters for several more minutes before setting the watch on the table before her. She grappled for the large photograph that held the image of two young girls.

"Your sisters," Candace offered. "Their names and ages are on the back."

As Rebecca peered into the faces of strangers, she felt a certain warmth wash through her like liquid sunlight.

Finally, flipping the photo over, she read the faded black ink on the back. It read, "Denise, age four," and "Danielle, fourteen."

"My sisters," she whispered.

The papers were copies of her birth records and adoption papers. The records held the physical descriptions, ages, and snippets of background information on her parents, but no names. As Rebecca's eyes scanned the page further, she read the descriptions of her grandparents, maternal and paternal, and other important relatives.

Then she reached for the quilt, faded and worn, with distinct images of dolls splattered over its face.

"They handed you to me wrapped in that quilt."

Rebecca suddenly realized this was the quilt her father had mentioned so many years ago.

Rebecca glanced at Candace briefly before lifting the quilt to her face, trying to decipher some faint scent of her mother from the overwhelming cedar aroma that steeped the blanket's fibers. When she could not, she placed the quilt against her chest and held it there with both hands, her gaze locked with Candace's. "Why are you giving me these?"

Candace shrugged gently. "I should have given them to you a long time ago and told you about your adoption, and what little I knew about your family."

Rebecca's eyes perked up. "You know my family?"

"Not really," Candace specified. "I knew a little about your mother and saw her at the hospital the day you were born. She's quite beautiful, you know."

"And my father?"

"Never got to meet your father. He was sick at the time, if I remember correctly. Don't know with what." Candace waved a hand through the air as though clearing a way through blinding fog. "Anyhow, he couldn't be there for the delivery."

Rebecca merely nodded, spellbound with the information being fed her, her senses lapping it up like a bear eating honey.

"But your mother," Candace smiled. "I remember her."

"What was she like?"

"Well, she was fiery, like you. Stubborn is more the word." Candace laughed openly, more out of respect than dislike.

Without realizing it, the corners of Rebecca's mouth tilted upward as she savored Candace's every word.

"She wouldn't let us have you right away, said she wanted to get to know you first." Candace shook her head. "Now that scared me. I thought that if she kept you even for the four days that she specified, she wouldn't be able to turn loose of you. But, she held to her bargain. On the afternoon of the fourth day, she handed you over to the adoption agency. The watch and the quilt came with you. The photo of your sisters was sent to you on your first birthday."

Rebecca lifted the photo and peered into the faces once again. "You gave her your address?" Surprise filled her tone.

"Not exactly," Candace admitted. "That was one of her stipulations: that she know who we were and where we lived. She wouldn't sign the papers if we didn't comply." She chuckled. "But we wanted you badly enough that we'd have complied with anything."

"Did she keep in touch?" Rebecca queried. *Could there be unopened letters and packages that Candace had never shared with her from years gone by?*

"Only once; on your first birthday. You see, I didn't want continued interference. Helena agreed."

"Helena."

"She asked only that she could send you something for your first birthday." Candace pointed toward the photograph. "She sent that. Otherwise, she never interfered with us. But she did ask one other thing."

"What?"

Candace hesitated a moment as though the words were too painful to utter. "She wanted us to tell you about her when you were old enough. She said that if you chose to seek her out, she'd be there waiting, and if you chose not to, she would understand. I'm sorry," Candace added hastily.

Rebecca's eyes no longer held flashing green anger. To Rebecca, Candace had truly changed. She was offering everything to her, even though Rebecca might still refuse to testify.

"I know you want to go to them. I can help."

Rebecca stood and smoothed her skirt. She stepped across the kitchen, rummaged through a drawer, then drew out a small pad of paper and a red ink pen. Returning to her seat, she handed these to Candace. "Write down what you know."

sixteen

The next morning, Rebecca slipped from the apartment an hour early without waking Candace. By creating some time by herself at the office, Rebecca hoped to begin the search for her birth family.

After parking the Porsche slightly crooked in the empty parking space, Rebecca dashed over to Candace's car to make certain everything was secure. It was.

When she reached the locked office door, she paused, thinking of Trevor. She hadn't had time to reflect on his reaction to her past. How did he feel about her now? Did he feel anything?

She couldn't deny her own feelings. After their first two meetings, she hadn't expected to care for the man at all, but over the weeks, as she'd observed the way he treated Heather and his clients, her feelings had changed. She had grown to love Trevor. When he'd looked at her in that special way at the hospital, she'd dared to hope he felt the same toward her. But that was before her sordid past had reared itself like an overgrown weed. If he no longer cared about her, she would turn and walk away, and never look back.

Rebecca jerked the key free and nudged the door open. After shrugging out of her rain parka, she stepped into Trevor's office, intent on making herself some hot coffee before settling down to work. Her feet froze. Trevor's office was a disaster!

Coffee cups and balled up papers were strewn all over, and pillows from the sofa lining the far wall had been tossed to the floor. A small, green striped pillow lay at the head of the sofa with a small indentation in its center, as though somebody had slept there.

She presumed the coffee cups were left over from the strategy meeting. Still, it wasn't like Trevor to leave a mess. One of the things she liked about him was his strong belief that every person had an obligation to clean up after himself.

Grudgingly, Rebecca busied herself with straightening up. It didn't take her long. After dumping soggy coffee grounds into the trash, she put on a fresh pot. All this cut into the time she had planned to use for her search.

Finally, with fresh coffee brewing, Rebecca wound her way back into her own office. She checked her watch. 7:30. She still had thirty minutes. She grasped her black clutch from the floor beside her, snapped it open, and pulled out the folded sheet of paper that held all the information she needed to begin her search. After popping the paper open, she laid it on the desk before her, smoothing it flat with her hands.

The red ink stood out on the white paper like an angel in the dark: *Lyle Warren and Helena Sue Lindley.* The last known home was listed as Pampa, Texas and the hospital's name was written across the bottom: Coronado Hospital.

Picking up the phone's receiver, Rebecca dialed the number for information. She gave the city and the name of the hospital. After scribbling down the number, she realized she had hardly breathed the whole time she was on the phone. It hadn't occurred to her how difficult this might be. She was deathly afraid.

For a moment, she thought of dropping the whole matter. After all, she certainly had enough to contend with. Why invite a whole new world into the picture? And besides, how did she know what her real parents would be like, other than what she had learned from Candace? Still, as though propelled by some unseen force, she placed her hand over the warm receiver and lifted it to her ear.

After punching the number for the hospital in Pampa, Rebecca waited for somebody to answer. On the second ring, she heard a soft voice fill the empty void.

"Coronado Hospital. This is Brenda."

Rebecca sucked in a shallow breath. "Uh. . .Hello. My name is Rebecca Wesbrook and I need some information."

"What can I help you with?" came the pleasant reply.

"W. . .well," stuttered Rebecca, "this may sound kind of strange, but I need to locate a person, a woman who had a baby on January 10, 1972."

"Do you have a name?" asked the woman on the other end.

"Yes, I do. Helena Lindley. Her husband's name is Lyle," Rebecca quickly added.

There was a slight pause. "Okay," the woman said finally. "I've got it written down, but I'm going to have to transfer you to records. Can you hold?"

"Yes."

Suddenly, the phone rang and a square light on the panel at the bottom of the phone flashed on and off next to the stable light that was Rebecca's call. Quickly, she pushed the button with her index finger.

"Hello," she said, then, realizing her goof, quickly covered by adding, "Trevor Houston and Associates."

"Oh, Rebecca. I'm so glad you're there," blurted Heather.

"Is something wrong?"

"No, I mean yes. It depends. Is Trevor there?"

Rebecca's heart thumped wildly in her chest. She must make a decision and fast. What if the lady at the hospital came back on the line?

"Listen, Heather, can I call you back?"

"Rebecca, Trevor never came home last night!"

Rebecca knew that the other call would have to wait. Her main concern was Trevor.

"That explains the couch," said Rebecca.

"What about the couch?" Heather's voice quaked.

"I think I know where he slept," offered Rebecca, "but I don't know where he is now. He certainly isn't here. How do you know he didn't come home last night? Sometimes, especially after a meeting, he's late."

"When I woke up this morning at six with the baby, I slipped past his room and he wasn't in bed. I switched the light on thinking he got up early, but his bed hadn't been touched."

"How strange," Rebecca voiced, more to herself than to Heather.

"I'm worried," said Heather. "This isn't like him."

"I know," Rebecca agreed. She was growing more anxious by the minute. The other call light went out, but Rebecca paid no attention to it.

"I'll do some checking and get back with you. If he shows up at the ranch, give me a call, okay?"

The line went dead.

Rebecca drummed her fingers against the desk's shiny wood. Did Trevor's disappearance have anything to do with her? Where could he be? And why hadn't he told anybody where he was going? This simply was not like Trevor. Had the news so repulsed him that he couldn't bear to face her again? She rested her head in her palms and prayed that wasn't the case.

After making a series of unsuccessful calls, it dawned on her. *Check his appointment book!* Trevor would never intentionally miss a scheduled appointment.

Rebecca jerked open the drawer to her left and pulled out the book. A quick perusal showed that the day was crammed with appointments. *Surely appointments he meant to keep,* thought Rebecca. But her eyes were riveted to the 8:00 A.M. section that had been crossed out with a giant X. Along its border, in tiny print, something had been written.

Squinting her eyes to see, Rebecca could barely make out an address and the unmistakable name *Martin.* Who was Martin?

She noticed the phone book's yellow pages opened an arm's length away and a business circled in red.

"Brian Martin," she read aloud. But her breath caught in her throat when she read the next few lines: *Therapist, sexual crime victims.*

Rebecca paced the floor with abrasive strides. It was one thing to be upset about the news, but quite another to go meddling into someone else's business!

She marched back to the chair, dropped into it, and punched Heather's telephone number.

After assuring Heather that Trevor was fine, she was kept on the line by a barrage of questions from Heather about his uncharacteristic behavior.

Rebecca was unwilling to go into detail, yet she didn't want to leave her friend hanging. "Look, Heather, I've gotta run. I've got a ton of filing and some phone calls to make. Can I get back with you?"

"How 'bout lunch?" offered Heather.

Rebecca hesitated. "You don't need to be out so soon do you? Anyway I was thinking about lunching in the office today."

"Tuna salad sandwiches okay?" Heather said with a chuckle. "My treat."

"Heather, don't try to come in. Honestly."

"Frankly, Rebecca, I could use the break."

Mentally reviewing her options, Rebecca concluded she'd better tell her friend the rest of her story before someone else got to her first. "Okay," she responded. "But be careful." The phone conversation ended.

In the following silence, Rebecca thought about going to the address listed beside Brian Martin's name, but decided against it. Why should she chase Trevor all over town? She already knew his motives. He thought she needed help, thought she needed therapy. What she needed was to be left alone. And when he did show up, she vowed, she would tell him exactly what she thought.

At five minutes to twelve, Heather staggered in, breathless from carrying the weight of the baby in its portable bed, a pink diaper-bag, and a wicker picnic basket loaded with food.

Rebecca immediately sought the child carrier and began cooing over her namesake. The baby only squirmed in its pink nightie, yawned copiously, and settled back to sleep. Rebecca looked crestfallen at Heather.

"That's all she does," Heather chuckled. "She only wakes when she's hungry or wet. Otherwise, we don't get to see much of each other."

After placing the carrier into a corner of the office and setting the food out, Rebecca bit hungrily into her sandwich, not realized until now how famished she was.

Heather paused over her sandwich to ask, "So, what's the news, the big secret that you couldn't divulge over the phone? I know it has to do with Trevor."

Rebecca suddenly lost her appetite. Her friend did have a right to know about Trevor, and yes, about her, too. She just hadn't expected things to happen as they did. She'd never intended to tell anyone what had happened. It was just too personal, too painful.

"Well, it's out in the open now," Rebecca said, taking a deep breath. "So I might as well tell you."

Rebecca stood and straightened the belt on her red shirt-dress. She paced the floor in front of Heather.

"Do you remember when I told you all about me when you were in the hospital?" she quizzed.

Heather nodded.

"Do you recall that I mentioned I might never tell you why I did what I did?"

"Yes, I remember."

"Well, you're about to find out."

seventeen

Rebecca finished with all she had to say. Her friend's stare made her feel uncomfortable. "You're making me feel like a freak."

Heather blinked hard several times. "I'm sorry," she offered. "You're not a freak at all. I just can't believe you went through all that and never told anybody. How?"

"I don't know," Rebecca confided. She knew her friend was not judging her and that helped.

Heather rose from her chair and knelt before Rebecca, taking Rebecca's hands in her own. "What will you do now?" Heather coaxed. "Will you testify?"

Retrieving her hands, Rebecca rose and stepped over to where the baby lay sleeping in its bed. She watched the infant for several minutes, even bent down to run a finger along its small silky brows.

"I don't know what to do," she finally admitted, still watching the sleeping infant. "I've thought about the baby, my mother's baby. How can I turn my back on that innocent child?"

"There's your answer. I know you, Rebecca. You'll do the right thing, even though it may be the hardest thing you may ever have to do in your life. Actually," Heather added, "I think you knew the answer all along. You're just afraid."

Silence filled the office until the only things that could be heard were the soft hum of the computer and the steady, sweet breaths of the sleeping baby.

Rebecca drew her own deep breath, expelling it loudly. "You're right," she conceded. "I have known what to do, but I *was* frightened. I'm *still* frightened."

Heather sat in the chair Rebecca had previously occupied. "If it's any consolation, I'll be right there with you."

Rebecca knew Heather meant well, but she realized she would have to handle this alone. Suddenly, the phone rang. Another client. "Looks like lunch is over."

After Heather struggled from the office with her load, the phone rang again. This time it was Trevor. The sound of his voice so startled Rebecca that for a moment she couldn't speak.

"Rebecca? You still there?"

Suddenly, she found her voice, and them some.

"I'm here all right! Where are *you*?"

"Wait a minute," Trevor explained. "I've had appointments."

Then as though remembering, he apologized for the mess. "I'll be by in a little while to straighten—"

Rebecca interrupted him. "Don't worry about that. I've already cleaned up. I want to know about that appointment!"

"I always have appointments, Rebecca," he volleyed.

"I want to know about the appointment with Brian Martin!"

Silence filled the receiver.

"I think we should talk about that," Trevor finally said in a tone less audible than normal.

She didn't reply.

"Rebecca, it's not what you think."

"Then what is it?"

"We don't need to discuss this over the phone. I'll be in the office in about an hour. Can we talk then?"

Her cheeks burned. She knew he would try to talk her into seeing a therapist and if she needed one at all, it was her decision entirely. She felt betrayed. Was this his idea of love? Or was he simply doing his duty as her boss? And nothing more? "No!" came her flat reply. "We will *not* talk about it!"

"Rebecca, wait—"

She heard his words trail off as she hung up, ending the conversation.

When Trevor did show up, Rebecca gave him no opportunity to explain. He muttered, "If that's the way you want it," and marched into his office, slamming the door behind him.

All Rebecca could think about was Candace's baby. She would do her best to protect the child from a man she knew was dangerous, but it didn't make things any easier.

Testifying about his alcoholism was one thing. Telling about a rape, in which she was the victim, was quite another. Shame swelled hot and vile inside of her. She grew angrier because of it. Feelings of helplessness overwhelmed her. Yet she knew she must let her story out no matter what the repercussions. Her suffering would be greater if an innocent child was put into the hands of a man as deplorable as Kane Wesbrook.

Trevor emerged from his office just as Rebecca completed the backup sequence for the files. He didn't say a word as he slung his black, pinstriped suit-coat over one shoulder and left.

Fine! She would be content if they *never* said another

word to each other. She had concluded a long time ago, after witnessing her mother and father's marriage, that if there was no trust in a relationship, there was *no* relationship.

Having completed her tasks, Rebecca tucked her rain parka under her arm and dug her keys out of her purse.

The morning fog had lifted around ten that morning, allowing the sun to warm things nicely. When Rebecca opened the door to her apartment, she was treated to the pleasant aroma of cinnamon potpourri. And when her eyes scanned the apartment, anything that had the potential to shine did just that.

Candace emerged from the hallway, a small hand-towel in one hand and furniture polish in the other.

"How did work go today?" she asked sweetly.

Scanning Candace's appearance, and the interior of the apartment, Rebecca was certain her mother had cleaned all day.

"I guess I could ask you the same question," she declared.

Candace burst out laughing. "I do know how to clean," she joked.

"Oh! I'm sorry," Rebecca apologized.

"There's no need for apologies," Candace offered without offense. She placed the can of polish on a table and draped the hand towel over it. "While you were growing up, the way you saw me was not the way I really am." She chuckled. "You may find that hard to believe."

Rebecca shook her head from side to side. "You're just different, that's all," she murmured. "So different."

"Bet you thought somebody like me could never change."

"Well, the thought had occurred to me," Rebecca offered truthfully.

Candace stepped over to the sofa in her bare feet and plopped down. She patted the cushion beside her and threw Rebecca a questioning glance. With only a slight hesitation, Rebecca took the seat by her adoptive mother.

"Believe it or not," Candace stated, "I had my own doubts."

"You did?"

"Certainly." Candace cleared her throat. "I knew what I was doing, Rebecca, but I didn't care." She searched Rebecca's eyes. "But, I do now. Do you believe that?"

Rebecca narrowed her gaze to the freshly vacuumed carpet. "I do believe that."

For a moment, neither said a word. Rebecca broke the silence. "I will testify."

Candace drew a choppy breath. "Are you sure?"

Rebecca nodded.

"Thank you," Candace offered. "I know how hard this must be."

"It wouldn't be right to allow a child to be placed into the hands of a man like Kane Wesbrook."

"Without your testimony, Rebecca, that's exactly where this baby will be." Candace rubbed at the dry skin on her hands. "My past is not pretty," she continued. "A judge would almost surely declare me an unfit mother. Kane would stand a better chance of gaining custody than I."

Rebecca's eyes widened with disbelief and Candace laughed.

"You wouldn't think so, would you?"

"No."

"He's got connections that I don't."

"But what about his drinking?"

Candace paused for a moment. "Yes, we could prove his drinking, but he's in a detoxification clinic right now, drying out. A judge will look favorably at that."

"And what about you? Have you quit drinking completely?"

"Yes," said Candace, "but not for the same reasons. I quit because I want a better life. Kane quit because he'll give up anything if he can get to me and your father." She flicked a delicate hand through the air, revealing fresh, clear polish on her nails.

She hesitated, then took Rebecca's hand. "So, you see. You're my only hope."

Rebecca smiled warmly as Candace called her lawyer with the good news, telling him that God was bringing a family together. This reminded Rebecca of her own need to locate her other family. Would God bring them together as well? She prayed He would.

eighteen

Another early morning mist shrouded the city as Rebecca wove her way to the office, clutching a black vinyl umbrella.

The office was dark and peaceful. Florescent lights burst with brightness as Rebecca flipped the switch by the door. After slipping out of her rain parka, she tugged at the short-cropped, white linen jacket she wore and smoothed it over the matching linen skirt before taking her usual place at the desk.

She located the scrap of paper containing the Pampa hospital number. Her hands trembled as she punched the sequence of numbers. She immediately asked for the records department and was greeted by a friendly, female voice. Rebecca identified herself.

"Yes, I remember," the woman offered.

"I'm sorry we got disconnected," Rebecca apologized. "An emergency came up, and I couldn't hold the line."

"That's no problem," the woman said. "As a matter of fact, I have the information you were needing."

"Great!" Rebecca's heart nearly leaped into her throat. "I've got pen and paper ready." But the silence on the other end dulled her excitement. "Is there a problem?" Rebecca probed.

"I just can't give that information out over the phone," came the voice. "There are certain channels you will have to go through to obtain this information."

A knot rose in Rebecca's throat. She was so close, and yet so far away. "Isn't there anything you can tell me?"

"Can I inquire as to why you need to locate this woman?" the voice asked. "You see, this information is confidential. We can't give out personal information to just anybody."

Rebecca drew a deep, exasperated breath. She understood completely, but wished, just once, they would make an exception. She answered the woman truthfully. "I'm Helena's daughter. I was adopted as an infant and I'm wanting to locate my birth family. I have strong reason to believe that they want to contact me also."

"Hmmm."

Rebecca heard paper shuffling on the other end of the line and a flicker of hope danced in her green eyes like a candle's flame. "I'll take anything you can offer me."

"I can't give you her address or phone number, but I can tell you this." There was a pause. "I'm looking in the city directory right now and I've found her name. It appears she still resides in Pampa. But, that's all I can tell you. The rest is up to you. If I were you, I'd make a trip to Pampa."

Breathless, Rebecca gave the woman her heartfelt thanks. With cautious steps, she entered Trevor's office and approached the front of his desk. She grasped the handle to the drawer that held many city directories Trevor kept on hand, never knowing when he would need an out-of-town number. The third directory from the top read "Pampa, Skellytown, Lefors."

For a moment, she clutched the book to her chest and closed her eyes, allowing the reality of it all to sink in.

After saying a silent prayer, she carried the book back into her own office and thumbed through the white pages until she came to the L's. She located LI, then LIND, and finally the name, "Lindley." There was only one Lindley listed.

Rebecca touched an index finger over the entry: *Lindley, Helena.* She held it there for a long moment before sliding it across the tiny dotted line to the telephone number. Then she studied the street address.

A phone call was not adequate for a meeting such as this, she surmised. She would meet her family face to face.

When Heather learned of Rebecca's good fortune, she insisted that the office phone calls be transferred to her home for the day. Rebecca left, feeling both excited and scared about what would transpire that afternoon.

She headed east, paying no mind to the tiny towns of Panhandle and White Deer she passed through. When the green road sign read *Pampa,* Rebecca's adrenaline shot through her veins like a cold IV. She was on the outskirts of a small city that had become the most important place in the world to her.

After stopping and asking for directions, she made her way through town to Banks Street. Rebecca looked from one row to the other of modest pier and beam homes, searching for the correct number.

When she found the right house, she pulled over and parked along the curb.

"Come on, Rebecca, you can do this," she said under her breath as her trembling fingers threaded through her long, dark curls. She wasn't sure whether it was relief or fear she felt when she saw the small, gray car parked in the dirt drive. Somebody might be home.

Before stepping from the security of her car, Rebecca studied the dwelling as though it were a person. She knew by experience that a home could tell a lot about its inhabitants.

The exterior of the home was covered with light bisque siding, trimmed in a grisaille of grays. Arborvitae shrubs lined the narrow walk leading to a small concrete porch. Thick ivy carpeted the flower beds on either side of the porch and wove their lanky vines up the sides of the house, giving it a more homey feel.

Taking one huge swallow and a deep, sustaining breath, Rebecca threw open the car door, stepped out, then shut it lightly.

Even the rap on the door was light. Suddenly, she wasn't sure she was doing the right thing. A host of scenarios bucked through her mind like mad bulls at a rodeo.

She suddenly spun around on her heel, intent on making it back to her car without being seen or heard. She had barely stepped off the porch when she heard the creak of an opening door behind her. A screen door flung open and a delicate voice questioned her before she had even turned around.

"Can I help you with something?"

Seconds seemed like hours as Rebecca fought to swallow the lump in her throat. She was certain it blocked her airway, causing the dizziness she felt. "I. . .I'm looking for Helena Lindley."

"I'm Helena," the woman said with a certain assurance to her tone that Rebecca immediately liked.

Haltingly, Rebecca closed the distance to the woman

and extended her trembling hand. "My name is Rebecca," she said. "Rebecca Wesbrook." She drew a deep breath and tried to keep her knees from shaking. "May I talk with you for a moment?"

The woman took a minute to scan Rebecca from head to toe, probably, Rebecca through, to analyze whether or not she could be trusted. This gave Rebecca the time she needed to analyze the woman whom she knew without a doubt was her mother.

Helena's crystalline, blue eyes danced with a gleam that told Rebecca she had conquered the hazards of life with grace. And her beauty remained untouched by time with its menagerie of trials and victories.

She wore white polyester pants and a matching tunic over her slim body. On her lapel, which Rebecca only now saw, was a pin that read *Helena Lindley, RN.*

Pride catapulted through Rebecca's body, only to be suddenly replaced with anxiety when she realized her mother might be heading to work. There was no way she could introduce herself if Helena would only have a few minutes to absorb the news before going to work. "Am I catching you at a bad time?" Rebecca queried, her tone almost pleading.

Helena cocked a quizzical glance at Rebecca and Rebecca hoped the woman wasn't annoyed with her evasiveness.

Drawing her left arm toward her eyes, Helena studied the watch on her wrist. "No," she finally answered.

Rebecca blew out a relieved breath that she caught halfway when saw the woman staring at her intently. She searched the houses surrounding them and hoped nosey neighbors were either napping or out shopping. It was obvious Helena wasn't going to invite her in. And why should she? Rebecca was, if only for the moment, a complete stranger to this woman. She bit at her bottom lip and smashed her hands together in front of her. "Helena," she struggled. "I. . .I'm your daughter."

Silence enveloped them like a shroud of darkness. Even the birds halted their songs as though sensing the moment's importance.

Finally, Helena moved, but only to grasp the wrought iron railing surrounding the tiny porch she stood on. Then with slow, cautious steps, she made her decent until she was face to face with Rebecca.

Rebecca dared not speak, or move, until Helena had spoken. She prayed that her mother's words would be filled with acceptance. Her fears were quickly allayed as she watched Helena's eyes brim with tears.

"Ragdoll," Helena choked, surrounding Rebecca's shoulders with arms, embracing her in a hug that had waited nearly two decadesto be born. "You look just like Lyle! Thank God I've found you." She laughed. "I mean, thank God you found me!"

Drawing relief from her own chuckle, Rebecca returned the embrace and they held each other and cried softly of unspent pain. Rebecca didn't care if anyone saw them. Their longing went so deep, it hardly yielded to the touch of a hug.

Finally, words escaped Rebecca's lips. "I'm glad I found you, too!"

Helena stepped away from Rebecca to get a better look at her. She touched her hand to her chest and shook her head in disbelief. "I can't believe how much you look like your father. It's almost as though he were standing before me."

"My father?"

"Oh yes!" Helena cried. "If you removed all that gorgeous hair, he would be here!"

"Is he—my—father here? Can I meet him?"

Dismay replaced the sparkle in Helena's eyes and Rebecca bristled. Hot tears swelled in her eyes and she somehow knew what was coming.

Helena touched Rebecca's shoulder. "I'm so sorry, child. Your father died when you were born." She dropped her gaze.

Rebecca touched her gently under the chin and lifted her eyes to meet her gaze again. "What took him?"

"Cancer. I'm sorry," she repeated.

Although Rebecca felt cheated, she didn't feel the wash of pain she would expect if her adoptive father were taken from her. . .or the way Trevor's absence tore at her heart. She had never known this man. "It's okay," she consoled and Helena smiled.

"I can still introduce you to him if you have the time."

"I have all day."

Helena stepped up onto the porch and opened the door. She motioned for Rebecca. The two women disappeared inside.

nineteen

"I held nothing back," Rebecca divulged that evening.

"How did she respond?" Heather quizzed as she cradled little Rebecca in her arms and nursed her.

There were alone in the office. Trevor was out of town on personal business and would call Heather when he arrived in New York.

"We cried a lot," Rebecca explained. "I think she feels partly responsible for my problems—thinking that if she hadn't given me up, none of this would be happening."

"What did you tell her?"

"I told her she did the best she could with what she had to deal with. She can't blame herself. *I* don't blame her."

"What else did you talk about?" Heather's blue eyes sparkled with curiosity.

"I learned what kind of a man my father was." Rebecca paused, reviewing old photographs and stories of him in her mind.

"He was a good man, a funny man, but a man with a lot of pride. I'm sorry I didn't get to know him."

"I'm sorry, too," Heather consoled. "But in a way, you are getting to know him. And now I know how to teach little Rebecca Diane about her daddy. Now, tell me about your mother."

"She kept me for four days and nursed me just like this." Rebecca stroked the nursing infant's head. "She's a strong woman, Heather, very strong."

Heather gazed lovingly into the baby's face, studying her tiny features. "That must have been hard on her, giving you up. I thank God for Trevor. His support allows me to give my baby the life she deserves. I couldn't imagine ever giving her up."

"We were poor. My father was dying. She's fought herself over that decision for eighteen years." Rebecca leaned back into the comfort of the sofa and draped one ankle over the other. "She wanted me to find her. That's why she never left Pampa."

"She never left because of you?"

Rebecca nodded.

"But what if you never came?"

"She told me she planned on dying in Pampa, even if I chose not to find her. I was her child and she never gave up hope." She paused. "That's the kind of love I hope to give my child someday," said Rebecca. She glanced at the baby, then drew her gaze back to Heather. "And Rebecca Diane, of course."

"What about your sisters?" Heather begged.

"You're as curious as an old cat!" Rebecca exclaimed.

"I know. But I can't stand it. This is so exciting!"

Rebecca held up a hand to thwart any more pleading. "Okay. Okay," she countered. "Denise, my older sister is away at Adams State College in Alamosa, Colorado. Actually, college has let out for the summer and she's busy harvesting potatoes for extra money before school begins again. She's studying to become a chemical engineer."

"A chemical engineer!"

"That's not the half of it!" Rebecca laughed. "Danielle,

my oldest sister, joined the Navy. She's a chief petty officer, stationed in Pensacola, Florida."

"Unbelievable! Even though Helena didn't have much, she certainly did a lot with what she had, especially her two daughters."

"I'm pretty proud of my sisters," Rebecca admitted, "but Helena's the one I'm really proud of. She overcame the odds."

"You can overcome the odds, too," Heather observed after a long silence. "You may look like your father, but you have Helena's spirit, Rebecca. You must see that God worked Helena's situation to good. And He can do the same for you."

"I'm beginning to believe that."

They laughed and talked for two more hours. Rebecca told Heather that Helena was planning a family reunion after Rebecca returned from testifying in Houston. Denise would drive up from Colorado after the harvest and Danielle would fly in as soon as she could get some leave.

❧

The Texas landscape spread out before her did nothing to pique Rebecca's senses. Her attention stayed glued to the red, glowing tail lights of Candace's white convertible as they shone through the hazy dusk. Only stopping to eat and fill up with gas, they made good time.

Rebecca was as frightened as a lost kitten at the prospect she faced. But she fought the fear with her growing faith. Then her thoughts would drift to Trevor, wondering how something like this could come between them.

"I think I could love you, Trevor," she whispered through trembling lips, the words dying within the confounds of the car. Yet, even saying the words, she knew nothing would ever come of them. Trevor was not the man she believed he was if he blamed her for what had happened. She had been violated, but she was still the same person.

The quivering in her stomach subsided somewhat when they pulled onto the circular, cobblestone drive that lead up to the Wesbrook Estate. As Rebecca stepped from the car, her eyes fixed on the garden. In full bloom and lit by well-placed flood lights, it reminded Rebecca of her father. Tears threatened. Where was he?

"Thank you, my God!" Maria exclaimed as she dashed from the mansion's well-lit entrance.

"Maria!" Rebecca cried as she caught her nanny in an embrace that said more than words ever could.

They separated only long enough to look into each other's eyes before embracing again. Finally, Maria spoke.

"You've come home, *niña.* No?"

"I've come home," Rebecca declared.

After settling into her old room, Rebecca grabbed a quick shower. The sumptuous smells of a Mexican feast beckoned her as she sailed down the sweeping staircase. In a way, she reasoned, it was good to be back, but in another way, she knew the estate was no longer her home. Amarillo was home.

After the meal, Rebecca helped Maria gather the dishes and leftover food. They made Candace lay down on the sitting-room sofa. After they had cleaned up, they joined her.

The women talked over all that had transpired since Candace first found Rebecca. Maria gripped Rebecca's hand when Rebecca confirmed that she would testify against Kane.

"It is a brave thing you do," Maria said. "I am very proud of you, *niña.*"

Rebecca squeezed Maria's hand. "This is something I must do. I know that now." She turned to Candace. "Are you worried about tomorrow?"

"Petrified."

"Me, too. What time do we need to be there?"

Candace sighed. "By 8:30 tomorrow morning."

Rebecca's gaze drifted to the Westminster grandfather clock standing stately against a nearby oak-paneled wall. It was already 10:00 P.M. "We probably should think about getting some rest. Tomorrow's a big day."

"I'm exhausted," Candace added, yawning and stretching cramped limbs. "I never realized pregnancy would take so much out of me."

A light chuckle moved through the women, a relief compared to the constant tension that had plagued them in the past.

Candace made her departure, leaving only Rebecca and Maria alone on the sofa. Maria moved to the coffee table and extracted a small white book from its drawer. She handed it to Rebecca. It was a small Bible, the one she had carried to church as a little girl, still in good condition, but definitely worn. Her gaze questioned Maria.

"I've marked a passage," Maria explained. "Don't read it now. Read it when you go to bed. It will help you sleep."

She bent her lips toward Rebecca's forehead and applied gentle pressure before removing them. Warmth flooded Rebecca's entire body at the gesture and a new sense of sleepiness replaced the tense exhaustion.

Making her way to her room, Rebecca decided to stop by Candace's room to check on her and, if she wasn't asleep, to tell her good night one more time.

But when she opened the door to the guest room her mother had used for years, her eyes scanned an empty bed. Baffled, she shuffled to the other side of the hall, where her father slept, and opened the door.

Rebecca smiled at the sleeping figure tossed in with the covers on the king-sized bed. She wound her way to her own bed.

After snuggling beneath the sheet, she opened the tiny Bible to the bookmark. Psalm 112:4 had been outlined in pink liner: "Unto the upright there arises light in the darkness; He is gracious, and full of compassion, and righteousness."

Rebecca fell asleep, the Bible still clutched in her hands.

twenty

The next morning, Rebecca was gently nudged awake. "Wake up, hon," Candace urged.

Sitting up, she asked hoarsely, "What time is it?"

"Six. We don't have much time. We can have some of Maria's hot blueberry muffins if we hurry." With that, she was gone.

Rebecca stumbled to the closet. She rifled through the jungle of clothes and chose a jade green, sleeveless turtleneck and a deeper green pleated skirt. After dressing, she wove her hair into a French twist.

Candace was already seated at the table when Rebecca arrived and she nodded her approval. Maria handed Rebecca a muffin.

Rebecca nibbled at the steaming muffin and sipped coffee from her cup. Although she wouldn't say so, she was anxious about what lay ahead.

By 7:30 Candace and Rebecca were seated in Candace's convertible. Before Candace reached for the ignition, she reached for Rebecca's hand.

"Your hand's cold," she admonished.

"Just nervous I guess."

"If you don't want to do this, you don't have to," Candace offered. "You can get out right now and I'll never say a word."

Rebecca searched her eyes. "I have to do this," she explained. "It's not just for you and the baby. It's for me as well. I have to do this for us."

Candace smiled, shifted the car into drive, and headed into downtown Houston.

The architecture of the two-story building, nestled among other more modest buildings, was strictly Victorian. Fine marble urns and fountains embellished lawn and flower beds outside the home-turned-office. Exquisite stained glass decorated the entrance door of the refurbished mansion.

Rebecca waited for Candace to join her and both walked up the steps together. Without a word, they stepped inside.

A thick, wood sign on a wall read *Veronica Chavez, Attorney at Law.* An arrow on the sign pointed in the direction of a wrought iron, spiral staircase. They ascended the stairs that ushered them into an elaborate waiting room. A pleasant musty scent greeted them as the secretary acknowledged their arrival.

"Wesbrook," Candace told the secretary who motioned them toward chairs upholstered in a floral chintz pattern.

"She'll be with you in a moment."

As Rebecca dropped into the overstuffed chair, she clasped her hands nervously in her lap. She could hear Candace's breathing over the secretary's keyboarding. She yanked a recent issue of *Home and Garden* from one of the marble table tops and tried to read an article, but her racing thoughts could not be diverted.

Candace chose to sit quietly and search their surroundings as though she were in a world of her own.

Rebecca knew Kane wasn't aware of her involvement in the case and wondered what his reaction would be.

Suddenly, voices drifted up from the bottom of the spiral staircase.

Her body tensed. One of the voices belonged to Kane; the other male voice she didn't recognize. The voices grew stronger as they ascended the stairs.

Placing a cool hand on Rebecca's forearm, Candace whispered, "Be strong."

Rebecca drew a deep breath and cast a steady gaze toward the entrance by the stairs.

Somehow, she hoped this day would never come. She would have been content if she never saw the man again. But, deep inside she knew life held no such promises. She must face her biggest fear: Kane Wesbrook. She wasn't going to drop her gaze to the floor when he strode in. She was going to stare him straight in the eye and take back the respect he had stolen from her.

The first man was dressed in a black pin-striped suit with matching tie. His hair was slicked back and its sheen matched the gloss of his black dress shoes.

Kane was right behind him, also dressed in a dark suit. His attention was focused on straightening his tie. His pant legs were a couple inches too long, causing him to look slumped. His hair had been hastily combed and when he caught Candace's gaze, Rebecca could see that his eyes were bulgy and bloodshot.

Either he was drunk, or he had a hangover, Rebecca didn't know. Either way, it was obvious he hadn't stopped drinking.

"Hello, Kane," Candace stated with stoic indifference.

Kane grinned maliciously and licked his lips like a lion about to devour a lamb. Suddenly all color drained from his face. Rebecca held his unwavering gaze for several seconds before Kane finally dropped his to the floor.

He turned to his attorney, who was talking quietly with the secretary, and caught his attention with a wave of his hand. He then rubbed furiously at his temples with thick fingers.

Rebecca felt her heart slow to normal. The worst was over. Let the rest happen as it would.

When Kane's attorney approached him, there was obvious concern in his expression. The attorney gripped Kane around the back with his long arm and led him off into a corner of the room. Rebecca and Candace watched as a series of tense words were exchanged. More than once, either the attorney or Kane would hazard a glance at Rebecca before engaging in testy conversation again.

Rebecca watched with obvious amusement as the tangled exchange went on for several more minutes before Kane's attorney approached the front desk.

"Tell Ms. Chavez that I need to speak with her immediately," he ordered.

The secretary removed her glasses, stood, and disappeared down the well-lit hallway.

Veronica Chavez, a petite woman of Mexican descent, appeared in the hallway.

"Yes?" she inquired of Kane's attorney.

"My client and I need a pre-disposition hearing, if that would be possible."

Veronica took a deep, exasperated breath. "I'm almost set up. Is this absolutely necessary?"

"Absolutely," said the attorney. Kane nodded in agreement. The three disappeared down the hall.

Rebecca cupped her hands over her nose and mouth

and breathed into them, feeling the hot, moist breath gather on her palms. Then she clasped them together in her lap.

"Are you doing okay?" Tears filled Candace's eyes.

Rebecca nodded weakly. She knew that whatever was going on had to do with her.

Suddenly, the three figures reappeared in the hall. Kane's attorney led the way, his expression stern. Kane looked ill, and Veronica radiated complete confidence.

Without a word or glance toward Rebecca and Candace, the two men filed down the stairs. When the entrance door slammed shut, Veronica approached Candace and Rebecca.

"Will you ladies come with me?" she asked before spinning on her heel and leading the way into a conference room. Candace and Rebecca followed, each lost in their own thoughts.

Rebecca took her seat in a brown leather chair, one of several that lined the table. A grandmotherly woman caught Rebecca's eye as she worked at one end of the table.

The woman was reinserting her dictating machine and its little stand back into its portable carrying case. She smiled warmly at the two new faces. Veronica approached the woman, whom Rebecca decided was the court reporter hired for the deposition.

Extending a petite hand, she offered her apologies. "I'm sorry you had to make the trip for nothing."

The woman gripped Veronica's hand with her own and offered a gentle shake before releasing it. "I'd rather it be resolved this way," she said. "The words exchanged during a child custody case can get pretty ugly. It's better when there are no words."

"Good luck," she said to Candace and Rebecca before thrusting her plump form through the doorway and closing the door behind her.

Veronica immediately took a seat opposite the women and made several notations on a yellow legal pad. Then she raised her dark eyes in Candace's direction. "I have some good news, Candace."

"Good news?"

"Yes." Veronica rested her small chin against the backs of her hands. "Mr. Kane Wesbrook has indicated that he would like to drop the lawsuit. His lawyer, Mr. Benton, will file a motion with the court tomorrow morning asking that it be dismissed."

"Did he say why?" Candace asked curiously, as Rebecca sighed in relief.

"He did not give a reason," Veronica explained. "All I know is that it's finished. You win by a stroke of luck."

Rebecca knew it had nothing to do with luck.

"What do I do now?" Candace queried.

Veronica smiled and stood. "Just have a healthy baby," she offered. "And let me know when you do."

Rebecca took the cue and stood on weak legs. Candace rose and, after a round of warm hand shakes, Candace and Rebecca hurried down the spiral staircase and out of the building.

The drive home was peppered with boisterous chatter about the baby and all the shopping excursions they would make to insure everything the baby needed was available. Finally they pulled onto the circular drive. Maria stood at the door, white towel dangling over one shoulder and her face beset with anguish.

Rebecca greeted her with open arms and a vigorous hug.

"What happened? Tell me what happened," Maria pleaded. "I cannot cook. I cannot clean. I cannot do nothing!"

Candace made her way around the car to where Rebecca and Maria stood. "It's okay, Maria. Everything's gonna be okay."

"It's true," added Rebecca soothingly. "He dropped the lawsuit." She giggled. "He took one look at me and dropped out of the whole affair."

"*Es verdad?* Is this the truth?" she asked Candace while using the towel to dab at tears that spilled from her eyes.

"It's all true," answered Candace, wiping at her own tears. "Our baby's gonna be okay."

Maria sighed with inexplicable delight, and then returned to her practical self. "You two must be exhausted. And hungry, no?"

"Exhausted, yes, but I don't think I could eat a bite, not right now anyhow," Rebecca answered. Candace echoed her sentiments.

"But we must celebrate this victory," Maria appealed. Her eyes crinkled up as though thinking. "I tell you what. I draw you both baths to help you relax. Then you meet me in the dining hall."

Candace rolled her shoulders. "A warm bath might do us both some good." She winked at Rebecca, who nodded.

Minutes later, Rebecca slipped beneath the frothy bubbles and luxuriated in the water's soothing warmth. She allowed her lids to close and concentrated on relaxing every muscle in her body, melting in the sensations.

For the first time in two months, she felt at peace with herself, her life. The only regret she had was losing Trevor. But she didn't blame him. And soon she would face him and tell him so. She wanted to talk it over, know his feelings. Trevor was worth it. She wouldn't let the past destroy the promise of what could be. She prayed he wouldn't either.

A knock sounded at the door. "Yes?" she called out.

"Rebecca," answered Candace. "Are you almost done? You have some guests waiting downstairs to see you."

Rebecca sat upright so fast that water and bubbles splashed over the edge of the tub, wetting the floor. *Guests?* "Who?"

She heard only silence in reply.

"Guests," she muttered to herself as she dressed. "Who could it possibly be? Friends from school?" She had just arrived. How could anyone find out that fast?

Candace was waiting with a smile that spanned her face. She had that sparkle in her eyes that Rebecca was still not used to.

"Who's here?" Rebecca whispered frantically.

Laying an arm around Rebecca's shoulders, Candace led her into the sitting room.

For a moment, Rebecca lost all ability to speak. There, on the sofa sat the one she was preparing to face. She just hadn't expected it to be this soon! Trevor!

Trevor rose and took both her hands in his. "Rebecca," he said. "I'm so glad I found you."

Rebecca found her voice. "W. . .wait a minute," she stammered. "I th. . .thought—"

"I know what you thought, Rebecca, and you were wrong. You never gave me a chance to explain."

"I'm willing to listen now."

Clearing his throat, Trevor began, "I didn't know how to help you, Rebecca," he offered, dropping his hand to his side and placing the other in his pocket. "I prayed about it so much I wore holes at my kneecaps. The only thing I do know is that I. . .I love you, Rebecca. I wanted to help you through this. The therapist seemed my only link."

"You wanted to help me?" Rebecca's chin quivered. "And what else did you say?"

Laughing, Trevor repeated what he knew she wanted to hear. "I love you. And I want to marry you. Nothing else matters."

She threw her arms around him and hugged him tightly. "I love you too, Trevor! And yes, I'll marry you!"

"Before you get too carried away, you'd better see to your other guest," Trevor gently reminded, releasing her. It was then she heard the name.

"Becca?"

She caught her breath in her throat, knowing only one person in the world called her that. Spinning on her heel, she saw him.

"Dad!" she cried, holding him to her.

"Don't you ever leave me again," he scolded, allowing unrestrained tears to streak his handsome face. "I don't care what happens, Becca. Don't you ever leave me again."

"I won't," Rebecca promised.

They held the embrace for a time longer before releasing each other. Then she turned to face Trevor and saw Candace and Maria standing near him. There was not a dry eye in the room.

"I won't leave you, Dad," Rebecca repeated with a twinkle in her eye, "until I marry this wonderful man."

"But, wait," she remembered as congratulations were given. "How did Maria and Candace find you, Dad?"

"They didn't. Trevor and some investigator friend of his did. I wasn't overseas; I was in New York. When you left, Becca, I couldn't stay in this old house one minute longer."

Rebecca cast an appreciative glance in Trevor's direction before giving her father another lingering embrace. So Trevor hadn't been avoiding her. He'd been looking for her dad.

"We must celebrate!" Maria broke in. Everybody burst out in laughter. She led them to the dining hall where bowls and spoons set the table.

"But, it's not lunch time, yet!" Rebecca gasped.

"This is no lunch," said Maria. "This is fiesta. She disappeared into the kitchen and returned with the largest tub of chocolate ice cream Rebecca had ever seen.

There was more laughter as places were found and Maria began dishing up the late morning treat.

"Let's celebrate!" Shane declared.

"How about a toast?" added Candace as she took Shane's hand in her own. Rebecca was relieved when he didn't remove it.

Rebecca raised a spoon filled with chocolate ice cream. "Here's to love, life, and family!"

"Here, here," everyone chimed in. "Here, here!"

A Letter To Our Readers

Dear Reader:

In order that we might better contribute to your reading enjoyment, we would appreciate your taking a few minutes to respond to the following questions. When completed, please return to the following:

Rebecca Germany, Editor
Heartsong Presents
P.O. Box 719
Uhrichsville, Ohio 44683

1. Did you enjoy reading *Ragdoll*?
   - ❑ Very much. I would like to see more books by this author!
   - ❑ Moderately
     I would have enjoyed it more if ____________

     ____

2. Are you a member of *Heartsong Presents*? Yes No
   If no, where did you purchase this book? __________

   ____

3. What influenced your decision to purchase this book? (Check those that apply.)
   - ❑ Cover
   - ❑ Back cover copy
   - ❑ Title
   - ❑ Friends
   - ❑ Publicity
   - ❑ Other ________________

4. On a scale from 1 (poor) to 10 (superior), please rate the following elements.

___Heroine ___Plot

___Hero ___Inspirational theme

___Setting ___Secondary characters

5. What settings would you like to see covered in *Heartsong Presents* books?

____

____

6. What are some inspirational themes you would like to see treated in future books?_______________

____

____

7. Would you be interested in reading other *Heartsong Presents* titles? ❑ Yes ❑ No

8. Please check your age range:
❑ Under 18 ❑ 18-24 ❑ 25-34
❑ 35-45 ❑ 46-55 ❑ Over 55

9. How many hours per week do you read? __________

Name _______________________________________
Occupation ___________________________________
Address _____________________________________
City ______________ State ______ Zip __________